LOVE IN PERIL

1792: Travelling on the long journey from London to Cornwall to meet her estranged father, Hester is plunged into peril when her coach is held up. She escapes and narrowly avoids falling victim to smugglers, due to the timely appearance of Hal Trevian. Hal takes her to her father, but, instead of finding security, other problems arise . . . although Hal is always there to support her. Will their interest in each other ever turn to love?

PHYLLIS MALLETT

◆————————————◆

LOVE IN PERIL

Complete and Unabridged

LINFORD
Leicester

First published in Great Britain in 2008

First Linford Edition
published 2013

British Library CIP Data

Mallett, Phyllis.
    Love in peril.- -(Linford romance library)
    1. Love stories.
    2. Large type books.
    I. Title II. Series
    823.9′2–dc23

    ISBN 978–1–4448–1398–2

Published by
F. A. Thorpe (Publishing)
Anstey, Leicestershire

1

Hester drowsed in eternal discomfort, unable to sleep properly because the coach jolted every time it hit a pot-hole in the winding coast road. The grating of the wheels was unceasing; the hard leather seat intolerable. She rubbed her eyes, wondering exactly where they were on the interminable trip from London to Cornwall — they had stopped for a change of horses in Plymouth during the afternoon, and were due to reach Polgarron around midnight.

It was May 1792 — when travelling was a great adventure in itself; fraught with many dangers. She could hear the coach driver's whip cracking monotonously as he urged the team to their best efforts, and tried to settle to sleep in order to pass the wearisome time until she should reach her destination.

Her thoughts meandered tiredly

along the well-worn paths in her mind and, even at this late hour, she was not certain that she was doing the right thing by going to her father in Polgarron. Mother had taken her to London from Cornwall when Hester had been four years old, and Father — Rufus Hendry — had become history, a shadowy figure in Hester's imagination that had been fed by Mother's malicious talk of him when her bad feelings rose to the surface of her hating mind.

But Mother had died of a fever three months ago and, Hester, now aged twenty-two, recalled the lawyer's dry as dust voice when he read Mother's will after the funeral.

'As your mother suggested, I have contacted your father, Rufus Hendry, of Polgarron in Cornwall, who charges me to settle your business here in London and, when the house is sold, to put you on the coach for Cornwall, where you will join him.'

Hester had written to her father, and

he replied offering her shelter in his home, but, to her sensitive mind, the general tone of his missive had bordered on unfriendliness, and doubts were raised in her mind which she would not ordinarily have ignored but having no-one else in the world to turn to, she had followed the lawyer's instructions, and was almost at the end of her long journey into the unknown.

A loud voice startled her, ringing out unexpectedly, and she stared up in surprise as the coach came to a halt so precipitately she was almost hurled to the floor. She regained her seat, rubbing an elbow, and lifted the canvas blind away from the glassless window of the coach to peer outside only to recoil in fright when a menacing figure leaned into the aperture and thrust a large pistol almost into her face. A masked face was behind the pistol, its eyes glittering malevolently through slits in some black material. Hester sank back on the hard-cushioned seat, shocked and frightened.

'Get out of the coach,' a harsh voice commanded. 'Be quick now and you won't be harmed.'

The door of the coach was jerked open and a strong hand reached in, grasped Hester's arm, and hauled her bodily out of the vehicle. Starlight reflected on the pistol in the highwayman's hand, and the attendant shadows added a touch of unreality to the nightmarish scene that confronted her keen gaze.

The driver and guard were sitting on their high seat, their hands raised, and a second highwayman was astride a horse by the heads of the coach horses, covering the driver and the guard with a brace of fearsome-looking pistols.

'Be quick and let us be gone,' snapped the highwayman beside the horses. 'What have you got in the coach?'

'Tis but a wench,' replied the man holding Hester's arm.

'Travelling alone? Leave her and grab the money box under the driver's seat.'

The highwayman released Hester

and stepped on to the front wheel of the coach to reach under the driver's seat, and at that moment a pistol blasted deafeningly and echoes fled away across the bleak landscape. The flash of the shot encompassed the highwayman reaching for the strong box, and he fell backwards from the coach with a cry of agony tearing from his throat. The second highwayman fired instantly, and the guard pitched forward to fall upon the backs of the team and thence to the ground.

Hester stood frozen in shock as the driver whipped the horses and the coach departed in a cloud of rising dust. The surviving highwayman fired an ineffective shot at the driver, then turned his horse and spurred away in pursuit of the coach. Soon the sound of the grating wheels and galloping hooves faded to nothing, and Hester found herself standing alone in the darkness, horror-stricken at being stranded in the middle of a hostile countryside.

Starlight provided some faint illumination to her shadowy surroundings. She shivered, for May this year was colder than normal, and a chill breeze was blowing across the sea from France. She could hear the sound of waves breaking on shingle somewhere to her left, and suppressed a shudder. A thin crescent moon was beginning to show on the horizon, and indistinct shadows reared up around her like ghastly ogres, threatening her with nightmarish menace.

She approached the sprawled figure of the highwayman on the pot-holed road and bent over him. Clearly, he was dead, and she shrank from touching him. The coach guard was dead also, lying with arms outflung. It was a hideous scene that impressed itself upon her mind, and panic flared in her breast.

The coach road stretched before her, following the line of the cliffs and showing eerily white in the gloom. Hester wrapped her cloak tightly around her slender body, and set out at a brisk pace, walking in the direction taken by the coach, fearful that the highwayman who had chased after the vehicle might return in a belated search for her, and the shadow of every bush seemed filled with uneasy menace.

The night appeared not so dark when her eyes became accustomed to it. The smell of the sea was in her nostrils as she strode out resolutely, following the pale ribbon of the road. She had no idea of her position, and could only follow the road. In fact, she began to relish the walk after so many hours spent in the confining coach. But she was fearful of being out at night in a strange place, and was keenly aware of her solitude.

The road bent to the left and descended a steep decline so suddenly that Hester had to lengthen her stride to maintain her balance, and was pulled forward by gravity until she was almost running. She found herself suddenly on the edge of a tall cliff that overlooked a cove where white water showed ghostly as it crashed against rocks far below her feet.

She paused to look around and, at that instant, a light flashed just out to sea beyond the big breakers. She frowned as she waited for it to show again, hardly able to believe her eyes, but the darkness remained complete, and she was puzzled, reasoning that the light could only have emanated from a darkened ship. A stark thought stabbed through her mind. Were smugglers at unlawful work?

She gazed long and steadily into the indistinctness of the night until her ears picked up the muffled sound of a boat's oars from out there in the dark void. The sound was cut off suddenly, and Hester shivered as cold air permeated through her clothes and chilled her skin.

She walked on only to stumble in an unseen pot-hole; almost fell, but recovering herself, was startled by a loud whistle that cut through the natural sounds of the night. She halted and looked around, and fear stabbed through her when she picked up the sound of heavy, scuffling footsteps coming along the road ahead. The night was too dark for her to see who or what was coming, and she eased to her right, seeing the dark shapes of bushes growing at the side of the road.

She tripped on an unseen grass verge and sprawled forward, bracing herself for an impact, but a pair of strong arms came out of the shadows and seized hold of her, clamping around her slim body like bands of iron. Before she could utter the cry of shock that started in her throat a hand was clamped over her mouth and she was held tightly in a strong embrace; could feel the warm breath of the stranger against her cold cheek.

'Don't make a sound,' a taut voice whispered in her ear. 'I'll not hurt you, but those men out there might kill us. We are both in danger, so stand still and don't struggle.'

Hester was unable to move. The arms were in an unbreakable grip around her, and the hand covering her mouth barely permitted her to breathe through her nose. She heard the footsteps on the road drawing closer, and suddenly there were others behind the first.

'What was it, George?' a harsh voice demanded. 'What alarmed ye? Is it the Revenue men?'

'I dunno. I saw a figure coming this way, and it didn't look like a man.'

'Mebbe it was the ghost of old Kate Twitchett,' another suggested with a snickering laugh. 'This is about where she went over the cliff in that gale last October, and they do say she haunts this stretch of road because she can't rest. Come on, there's no-one about. The Revenue men should be looking for us on the other side of Polgarron. Let's get a drink of rum and start moving the goods to clear the coast before the sun comes up.'

Three men turned and went back the way they had come, their figures

10

growing indistinct and then fading completely. The hand covering Hester's mouth relaxed its grip a fraction.

'You won't scream if I take my hand away, will you?' her captor demanded.

Hester shook her head and the hand was withdrawn carefully. She drew a deep breath. Her heart was pounding and she was badly shocked. The arms about her remained in place, holding her tightly against a hard anonymous body.

'I'm sorry I had to treat you so roughly,' the voice continued in her ear, 'but there was little time to get you under cover. If those men had caught you they would have flung you off the cliff into the sea, as they probably did Kate Twitchett, and I would have followed you into the cove just as quickly if they'd clapped eyes on me. It would have been a case of being in the wrong place at the wrong time.'

'Who are they?' Hester asked.

'I'll not mention names.' He laughed grimly. 'It's better you don't know.'

'Then who are you?' Hester could see

none of the personal details of her apparent saviour. His face was just a pale blur in the night and his strong figure bulked large in the shadows.

'Hal Trevian, Miss, and who are you, wandering out here alone in the dark?'

'I'm Hester Brandon. I was on the Polgarron coach.' She recounted the incident of the attempted robbery. 'And may I ask what you are doing out here at this time of the night?'

'I was riding home from business in Plymouth when my horse threw me and bolted, and I was making the long walk to Polgarron when I saw lights in the cove below and heard the sound of smugglers unloading a lugger. I heard their look-out walking this way just as I spotted you coming. You were making the devil of a noise, tripping and gasping, and it looked at one moment as if you might fall over the cliff. The smugglers must have heard you coming a mile away.'

'The road is full of potholes,' Hester

protested, 'and I have never traversed it before. It slopes very steeply just back there, and compelled me to run against my will.'

'That's probably what happened to old Kate last year. I don't recognise your voice. You must be a stranger to Polgarron.'

'You could say that. I was born there years ago, but my mother took me to London and I never saw my father again. Mother died three months ago so I am returning home at long last.'

'There's no man named Brandon in Polgarron. Are you sure you're going to the right place?'

'Brandon was my mother's maiden name. My father is Rufus Hendry of Tregowarth.'

'Rufus Hendry!' Trevian spoke in somewhat awed tone.

'Why do you say his name in such a manner?' Hester demanded. Danger seemed to have sharpened her senses.

'No reason beyond natural surprise.' His answer was smooth and immediate.

'I wasn't aware Rufus Hendry had ever married. Thank Heaven I was on hand when you arrived. It would have been a tragedy if the smugglers had caught and disposed of you. Does Rufus know you are about to visit him?'

'He knows I shall be arriving, but not exactly when.' Hester spoke dubiously, suddenly afraid that she would not, after all, be welcomed by her father and, at that moment, she was sorry that she decided to come to Cornwall.

'And the coach was held up, by Jack Savage, no doubt. You've made a poor start to your visit, Miss Brandon, but your circumstances should improve rapidly because Tregowarth is this side of Polgarron, not far inland from here, and I'll see you to Rufus Hendry's door. The house is barely a mile from this very spot.'

'That's a relief, and it is very good of you to go out of your way,' Hester replied. 'Perhaps you will be able to borrow a horse from my father. It would save you some steps after your own adventure.'

'I'm willing to try my luck at Tregowarth, but many a man who lives around here would avoid approaching the place unannounced and in the dark. We'd better bide awhile or we might run into the heels of those smugglers, and that would set us on another adventure that would probably see the end of us.'

Hester suppressed a shiver. The night air was cold and the crashing waves on the rocks in the cove below sounded hostile. She felt as if she had suddenly awakened into a nightmare that had no ending. She had heard that Polgarron was a quiet little harbour on the Cornish coast overlooking the mouth of the English Channel, and had expected to find its inhabitants going quietly about their business — and perhaps that was the order of things during daylight hours, but nightfall brought its own nefarious activities, and she hesitated to allow her mind to pursue those implications.

Hal Trevian took hold of Hester's hand and led her along the road, moving slowly through the night. The sea spray was moist against Hester's face as she peered around anxiously, wondering if the smugglers had gone, although no unnatural sounds broke the heavy silence. They turned at length into the bushes at the side of the road to ascend a well-worn footpath over rough ground, and she was breathless by the time they reached an undulating crest and paused to regain their breath.

'We should be safe now,' Trevian remarked.

The moon was now well clear of the horizon and shed silvery light over the mysterious landscape. Hester peered out over the cliffs and could see white water flying over rocks. The sea itself was dark and mysterious, the night concealing any craft that happened to be abroad, whatever its business.

'It's a beautiful sight in daylight,' Trevian continued. 'Do you remember anything about this place from when you lived here?'

'No, I was much too young when Mother took me away.'

'Well, I hope you will like it, although I suspect there are many surprises for you if you decide to stay.'

'Why do you say that?'

'It's just an observation.' He laughed easily. 'Life in London is very different from how it is in this part of the world.'

'Smugglers, for one thing, and highwaymen,' she countered.

'You should not come up against them every day. I expect your father will keep a very sharp eye on you after he learns of your experiences this night. Come along, the going will be much easier from now on. I expect you are very tired after your long journey.'

He set off along a rough path that led inland and Hester followed closely, holding his arm fearfully, unable to make much of her surroundings. The sound of the sea lessened a great deal as they moved inland from the cliffs until it was just a faint muttering in the background, and soon the rough, bushy ground gave way to level grazing land, and once, Hester heard sheep bleating plaintively somewhere close by, the sound echoing eerily in the night. A sigh escaped her as a house materialised out of the shadows.

'Tregowarth,' Trevian said. 'I hope you'll be very happy here, Miss Brandon.'

'Thank you.' Hester could feel exhaustion seeping into her body with the realisation that she had finally reached her destination. A dog barked somewhere close by when Trevian opened a gate. Hester staggered, and Trevian caught her elbow and steadied her.

'I hope you won't judge Cornwall by your recent adventure,' he remarked as they walked along a gravelled path towards the house, approaching from the right and at an angle to the main entrance. 'Look, there's a coach turning in at the main gate. It looks as if Rufus has been to Polgarron to meet you.'

'He wouldn't have known exactly when I should be arriving.' Hester could feel tension building up inside her now the moment of meeting her father was at hand. They were strangers, and she realised that she had an unfavourable image of him in her mind because of the way her mother had always spoken of him. Arrogance and selfishness were but two of the string of insults Mother had never failed to use.

The lamps on the coach marked the progress of the vehicle to the front door of the mansion and, as they drew nearer along the path, Hester saw two figures alight from the coach and mount the steps to the front door, which opened at their approach, allowing a great shaft of yellow light to encompass them.

'That's your father,' Hal Trevian said. 'You can tell him anywhere, for there is none taller than Rufus in these parts.'

Hester felt suddenly faint with anticipation. Trevian sensed her condition and tightened his grip on her elbow. Hester stumbled as a black wave swept up from inside her as all the fears and doubts of the past weeks reared up into the forefront of her mind, and she pitched soundlessly into the great encompassing pit that seemed to open up at her faltering feet.

2

Hester was only dimly aware of being lifted and carried up the dozen steps leading to the front door of Tregowarth. Hal Trevian kicked the door with his foot, and Hester forced herself to summon up some semblance of strength as she heard heavy bolts being withdrawn on the inside of the massive door. Trevian set her feet on the ground and slid an arm around her waist to support her, and Hester tried to stand unaided as the door was opened and a shaft of light emerged from the interior of the house to encompass them in yellow brilliance.

The light dazzled Hester and she lifted a hand to shield her eyes.

'What's this?' demanded a harsh voice. 'Here's Hal Trevian on my doorstep with a wench in his arms!' Coarse laughter echoed. 'Haven't you mistaken Tregowarth for The Eel Pot

Tavern in Polgarron?'

'Do enjoy your joke, Rufus,' Trevian replied sharply. 'Your jesting will turn to anger when you learn that this is your daughter from London. She was on the coach from Plymouth, which was held up near Tredgett Cove, and then she almost ran into smugglers coming ashore in the cove. It was fortunate I happened to be on hand to save her, and I've brought her home.'

A smothered curse sounded. Hester blinked, and her gaze slipped into focus as she looked at the huge figure standing in the doorway. Her father was tall and powerful, with narrowed blue eyes staring from an angular face. His grimly-set mouth was an uncompromising line in his countenance, and his large nose looked as if it had once been broken and then badly set. His long, reddish hair needed combing. He must have been a very handsome man in his youth, Hester surmised, but the passing years had exacted a toll on his looks

22

and now he was set on a decline into middle age.

'Hester?' Rufus reached out a great paw of a hand and grasped Hester's arm.

'Father!' Hester was aware that her senses were beginning to gyrate again, and tried to steel herself against her rioting emotions. She was drawn across the threshold of the house in which she had been born, and her legs became weak and threatened to betray her. She looked up into her father's pale eyes, mesmerised by his bulk and power and wondered why her mother had fled to London all those years before.

'Come and sit down. You look worn out. I expected to collect you from Polgarron in the morning. I left word there that you were to be put up at the inn when the coach arrived. Trevian, I owe you my eternal thanks for taking the trouble to see Hester home. How did you happen to be on the scene when you met her? Were you watching the smugglers?'

'Heaven forbid! I was returning from business in Plymouth when my horse threw me near Tredgett Cove and bolted. I was walking to Polgarron when I heard the smugglers, and thought it was wise to hide until they had gone. Then Hester came along the coast road and the smugglers heard her, but I managed to get her into cover before she was discovered.'

Hester sat down on a chair in the entrance hall. She was curious about the man who had saved her, and looked at him as he came to stand before her. Until now he had been just a disembodied voice in the night, and her interest quickened as her gaze rested on his tall, lean figure.

She judged him to be in his middle twenties. He was dark-haired, with brown eyes that peered concernedly at her. His clothes were well cut and could only have come from London, she thought. He was pleasing to her gaze, having the look of a gentleman about him; was well-spoken, and quite handsome. She wondered what he did for a living, for his hands were soft and white.

Trevian, in his turn, gazed intently at Hester upon seeing her for the first time, and his eyes became alive with interest.

'Miss Brandon,' he said, a ghost of a smile playing on his lips. 'I had thought, judging by the sound of your voice, that you were a fairy beauty, but my assumption did you a grave injustice. My apologies for thinking you were merely beautiful. Your loveliness exceeds my imagination.'

'Cut out that kind of talk,' Rufus Hendry said harshly. 'Can't you see she is near to exhaustion? Call again another day to pay your respects, if you wish, Trevian, but now you should leave. If you are afoot then you can borrow a horse from my stable.'

'Thank you, Rufus. I'll avail myself of your offer. Goodnight, Miss Brandon. I hope I may call on you soon, to enquire after your health, and I trust your adventure tonight will have no ill effects on you.'

'Thank you, Mr Trevian,' Hester replied. 'I thank God you were there when I needed rescuing.'

'All's well that ends well,' he responded, as he departed in the company of a tall man dressed in sombre black clothes, who had remained in the background during Hester's arrival.

Hester experienced a sense of disappointment when the big front door closed behind Hal Trevian. She had suffered an ordeal bordering upon a nightmare, and realised that she was suffering from shock, but she could still feel the imprint of Hal Trevian's arms around her when he had held her on the cliff top, and his effect on her was just like that of a glass of sparkling wine — she was filled with an impression of excitement and wonder.

'The coach, Father,' she said faintly. 'The guard and one of the two highwaymen were shot, and both lay dead on the road. The driver whipped the horses and fled, leaving me stranded, and the second highwayman chased after the coach.'

'Try not to think of it,' Rufus boomed in his deep voice. 'It comes to a pretty pass when honest folk cannot go about their lives without being harassed by bad men. We are blighted by a local highwayman, Jack Savage, and there will be no peace for any of us until he is caught and hanged. God knows the authorities have had their chances to rid us of his company, but Savage is as slippery as an eel. But now you must rest. A room has been prepared for your arrival, and a good night's sleep should pull you together.'

An old woman, dressed in black, and with a shawl over her grey head, came limping forward from the uncertain shadows around an inner door to the left. Her face was lined by her years, but her dark eyes seemed ageless, gleaming from the nests of wrinkles surrounding them. An over-long nose and a pointed chin gave her ancient face a witch-like appearance.

'Agatha is the housekeeper,' Rufus

said. 'This is my daughter, Hester, so take good care of her, Aggie. It seems she has suffered an ordeal getting here. Attend to her needs and then put her to bed.'

'I know who she is!' Agatha replied sharply. 'Do you think I had forgotten her? I nursed her when she was but a babe, and it was a scandal that she was ever taken from here. Come with me, Miss Hester, and I'll care for you. I never thought to see the day that would bring you back to this sad house.'

'Don't go filling her head with your nonsense, you harridan, or you and I will fall out,' Rufus warned. 'You're not so old that you can't be turned out of doors, so take heed. If you go against my wishes, as you usually do, I shall be greatly annoyed.'

'I hear nothing but a dog barking at shadows,' Agatha replied. She pushed by Rufus and took Hester's arm. 'Come away to my kitchen and I'll tend to your needs, my dear. I'll have your bed warmed — sleep is the best cure for what ails ye now. You have been away from your home far too long, but here you are at last, and we shall see what we shall see.'

'Sleep well,' Rufus boomed. 'We'll talk again in the morning, Hester. You will have a good life here, I promise you.'

Agatha held Hester's arm, clutching it as if afraid her charge would suddenly vanish. They crossed the hall, passing a wide staircase that led to the upper regions of the big house, and traversed a short passage that gave access to the rear of the building to enter a large kitchen, where a cosy fire burned in the grate of a large cooking range.

'Come along, my pretty. I'll let no harm come to you. Your poor mother never liked Tregowarth, although she tried hard to settle here. Rufus Hendry is a difficult man to live with these days, but he was impossible as a young man. Your mother did her best, God rest her soul, but she did not belong in this life and could not adjust no matter how she tried. I was sorry to hear of her passing, and I hope she has gone to a better life than she ever found here.'

'I have a vague recollection of you,' Hester said uncertainly, her memory set into motion by Agatha's voice and appearance. 'I was very young when Mother took me away to London, but I do recall you.'

'And so you should, my dear. I nursed you when your poor mother was abed with her sickness. She was too delicate for this rough household, and her life was worried out of her by the ways of her husband. Come and sit by the fire while I attend to your room. Are you famished after your long journey? Is there anything I can get you?'

'No, thank you. I desire nothing but a bed.' Hester was beginning to feel a nervous reaction to her recent experience.

Agatha led her to a seat by the fire and fussed around her until the man who had escorted Hal Trevian to the stable entered the kitchen and came to stand before Hester. His dark eyes showed concern as he looked at her.

'This is my husband, Edmund,' Agatha introduced. 'We came here as young folk to run this house for your grandfather, now long dead and, although we never planned to stay more than a few years, our fate settled us in a different direction, and now we are resigned to the fact that we shall never leave. Over all the years that have passed, your mother was the only person to leave Tregowarth and remain clear. Even you have returned, and when you left with your mother you were much too young to feel the pull Tregowarth has on everyone who spends a night under its roof.'

'I remember your mother well, Miss Hester,' Edmund said in a low voice. His fleshy face was lined and his dark eyes were narrowed and glistening in the lamplight. 'I like to think that I had a hand in her decision to leave, and I prayed that she would never be forced to return.'

'Why was my mother unhappy here?' Hester asked. 'Did my father ill-treat her? She never talked about her life here, but she did not have one good word to say about my father.'

'Let the past rest, dear,' Agatha said. 'You had no choice but to return, and we shall watch over you until you marry and depart.'

Hester's thoughts were in turmoil, and shock enveloped her, but she thrust away the cloud of doubt that assailed her mind.

'Agatha, take the warming pan to Miss Hester's room,' Edmund said. 'Can't you see she is exhausted? Get her to bed before she suffers from the effects of her ordeal. She has had a bad welcome to this house, and she needs to get off on the right foot to find any happiness here.'

Agatha turned and scuttled away. Hester closed her eyes. The heat from the fire warmed her frozen body and comfort returned slowly to her limbs. Edmund sat down opposite, and she could feel his strong presence although he did not speak. She heard Agatha moving around in the background and, lulled by the warmth of the big kitchen, began to drowse, only to be jerked back to reality minutes later by the noisy opening of the kitchen door. She sat upright in the chair and opened her eyes.

Agatha was returning, carrying a long-handled warming pan.

'I was hoping to get Miss Hester into her bedroom before Willard came home like the bad penny he is,' Agatha remarked to Edmund. 'But he has just walked in, and is asking to see Miss Hester. Shall we take her up the back stairs?'

'It will be better for her to meet him down here,' Edmund replied. 'I'll go and see if there's anything he wants while you take her up.'

'Who is Willard?' Hester asked as Agatha grasped her arm and almost dragged her from the chair.

'The master pulled Willard Cooper

from the sea in a storm when the wreckers were doing their murderous business on Porleston Point,' Edmund responded. 'Willard was twelve years old at the time, which was twelve years ago, and he's lived at Tregowarth ever since. The master looks upon him as the son he never had in marriage, and Willard certainly acts as if he has Hendry blood in him.'

Edmund arose and departed, looking like a tall crow in his black clothes. Hester glanced questioningly at Agatha, who held her wrist in an inflexible grip.

'It's all right, child,' Agatha soothed, leading Hester to the door. 'You will meet Willard tomorrow, but tonight you should be free of his attention.

At that moment Hester was too tired to care about Willard Cooper or anyone else, but her curiosity was aroused by Agatha's words and a thrill of anticipation filtered through her breast as they went along the passage to the hall.

Edmund's tall figure was disappearing through a doorway on the left, and

Agatha scuttled forward like a black beetle, her shoes making insistent rapping sounds on the stone floor. Hester hurried along, almost running to keep abreast, her wrist imprisoned in the housekeeper's tight grasp as if she were a recalcitrant child.

Agatha paused and went on tip-toes past the doorway of the room Edmund had entered, and Hester felt her curiosity burgeoning.

Once past the doorway, Agatha set off again, but they had barely reached the bottom of the staircase when a loud voice called out peremptorily. 'Not so fast, Agatha. What's your hurry? If that is Hester you're bundling up the stairs then hold on. I expressed a wish to see her. I'm very curious about young Hester.'

A pang stabbed through Hester's breast as she turned on the bottom step to face the speaker. She was intrigued by his voice, which, although undoubtedly masculine, was pitched slightly higher than was normal for a man, and registered in Hester's ears as one she had certainly heard before.

She saw a tall, lean man, dressed in a dark topcoat, a tall black hat, and brown riding boots, striding towards her. He had wide shoulders and looked very fit, but it was his face that held her attention, particularly his dark eyes. They were filled with a harsh expression, and were very bright, as if fed by an inner passion. His face was angular, his forehead broad, his nose long above a wide mouth, and he was handsome in a foreboding way. He was smiling, but there was something about his lips that belied the smile.

Hester suppressed a shiver at her first sight of him, while her subconscious mind thrust up speculations about his voice. It was impossible that she had heard it before as they had just met, but the impression remained in her mind.

'So you are Hester!' Willard paused before her, and although Hester was standing on the bottom stair she barely reached up to his shoulder. He grasped her hand and shook it vigorously. 'How do you do, Hester? Has Agatha told you yet about me? I'm Willard Cooper. I came here in a storm about twelve years ago. I run the estate these days, with Rufus taking time off for more leisurely pursuits. I heard that you were on the coach that was held up earlier this evening.'

'I suffered that misfortune,' Hester replied.

'Tell me about it,' Willard pressed.

Hester recounted her experience, feeling like a trapped rabbit under Willard's firm gaze. She was aware that she gabbled slightly, her thoughts in turmoil because she found his high-pitched voice somewhat familiar.

'So, one of the highwaymen was shot dead!' Willard observed when she fell silent. 'Not Jack Savage, I'll be bound. He has the luck of the Devil! And you were left when the coach took off, and then fell into the path of smugglers coming ashore in Tredgett Cove. Thank Heaven Hal Trevian was on hand to see you through. You've had a lucky escape, Hester, and I hope the experience won't discolour your first impressions of Cornwall.'

'She will feel much better after a good night's rest,' Agatha said sharply. 'The poor girl is almost asleep on her feet.'

'I shall look forward to talking with you on the morrow.' Willard smiled expansively and turned swiftly, his boots rapping on the flagstones as he returned to the room from whence he came. 'Goodnight, Hester,' he called over his shoulder. 'Sleep well.'

Hester half-stumbled as she turned to resume ascending the wide stairs, her thoughts taken up with the sound of Willard's voice. It had sounded familiar, despite the fact that she was aware of being among strangers here.

She could recall Hal Trevian's voice quite clearly, and the voice of one of the smugglers who had almost accosted her at the cove was also clearly defined in her memory, but Willard's voice remained in the limbo of her inner thoughts and she could not recall why it sounded so intriguing.

'I don't like Willard,' Agatha said in a fierce undertone as they reached the top of the stairs. 'Everyone detests him. He acts like he owns Tregowarth. He's an upstart, and cruel. You've only got to look at his mouth to tell what kind of a man he is. I've witnessed many instances of his cruelty over the years, and if you'll be warned by me, Miss Hester, you'll keep him at a distance.

'That one has deep thoughts and dark intentions, and was most likely spawned by the Devil, and I wouldn't trust him out of my sight. Take heed of my words, for I know what I am talking about.'

Hester was startled because her thoughts had been running in similar fashion. In her estimation, Willard could not to be trusted under any circumstance.

'I hope you will like the bedroom we have prepared for you,' Agatha resumed as they walked along a gloomy passage.

'I'm sure I shall.' Hester felt so exhausted she would not have cared if she found herself in a kennel in the back yard.

She followed Agatha into a large room which was pleasantly decorated in pale green furnishings, but was hardly able to take note of her surroundings, and went through the motions of preparing to retire for the night with nothing but the longing to sleep uppermost in her mind. When she finally tumbled into the warm bed she murmured a goodnight to Agatha and fell asleep almost instantly despite her nervousness, telling herself that tomorrow was another day in which to come to terms with her new life in Cornwall . . .

3

Sunshine probing through a narrow gap in the heavy curtains brought Hester slowly out of the blessed realms of sleep to find daylight filtering into her room. She looked around at the unfamiliar setting while her mind recalled the incidents that had attended her arrival the night before. Much refreshed by her rest, she stretched and sat up, and then slipped out of the bed and went to the window to peer out curiously over the nearby cliffs at an expanse of calm sea glittering in the early morning sunlight.

She could hear the muted roar of waves crashing against rocks on the shore, but the broad sweep of the Channel was serene in the beautiful May morning; merely caressed by the gentle breeze that stirred the grass along the cliff top. Hester liked what she saw, and a thrill of anticipation suffused her as she turned away from the scene to dress, impatient to go out and explore.

The big house was silent as she descended the staircase, but early as it undoubtedly was, Edmund appeared in the hall as she went to the front door.

'Good morning, Miss Hester,' he greeted. 'You are up early. Couldn't you sleep?'

'Good morning, Edmund. I slept very well, thank you. But I am an early riser from habit, and I'm keen to take my first look at the Cornish scenery.'

Edmund smiled and opened the door for her.

'Don't go too far,' he warned. 'The master expressed a wish to see you first thing this morning. Breakfast will be ready in an hour. And one word of warning, don't go too close to the edge of the cliffs.'

'I shall be very careful,' she responded, and hurried out of the house as if escaping from a prison, her thoughts discoloured by the coach hold-up and her close escape from the smugglers.

Descending the steps leading to the greensward beyond the terrace, Hester turned to get her first glimpse of Tregowarth, for it had been cloaked in darkness when she arrived the night before and she had been denied any details.

The house rose up three storeys, and was sited almost at the top of a wooded ridge that obviously protected it from any storm coming from the east across the Channel. Red brick walls, mellowed by age and gapped by many tall windows, were topped by a dull grey slate roof and tall chimneys. Ivy infested the building, and had grown halfway across some of the windows. Elms and poplars acted as wind breaks, and the countryside stretched away in all directions.

The roar of breaking waves intrigued her, especially as she could see the calm waters of the Channel glistening passively in the sunlight. Presently she reached the top of the cliffs, and paused almost on the very edge to look down at the narrow shore where black rocks, looking like crouching lions, were under siege by waves that beat sullenly and earnestly against the obdurate citadel of the cliffs. Spray flew in the sunlight, and Hester suppressed a shiver as she recalled the night before, when she had almost blundered into the smugglers.

Thank Heaven Hal Trevian had been on hand to help her. An image of Hal's face appeared in her mind, and she became aware of an eagerness to meet him again, for she could still feel the imprint of his strong arms around her and feel his warm breath against her cheek.

However the same was not true about Willard Cooper. Apart from the fact that his voice intrigued her, she had sensed an undercurrent in his manner that held her feelings remote and distant. Her instincts warned against him, and she felt confused by her attitude without knowing the reason why.

Her father was an enigma. Mother had never discussed him, or given any reason why she fled to London from Cornwall all those years before. Agatha and Edmund had hinted at marital difficulties, but Hester sensed that she would get only one side of the story from them.

She walked along the cliff top, and was careful to remain at a safe distance from the sheer drop to the shore. The tide was ebbing, and a thin strip of white sand lay exposed beyond the jumbled rocks at the foot of the cliffs. She wondered if there was a way down to the shore, but could not see even a footpath in evidence.

The sound of hooves pounding the grass startled Hester, for she was absorbed by her surroundings and had lost all track of time. She turned to see a rider coming towards her from the direction of Tregowarth, and frowned when she recognised Willard. He approached at a gallop on a powerful black stallion, and reined in only feet from her, coming so close that she instinctively moved aside for fear of being ridden down.

'You're an early bird,' Willard smiled as he dismounted, although his narrowed gaze seemed devoid of humour. 'Rufus has been asking for you, and became concerned when Edmund said you'd left the house. This is not London, you know, and a girl out alone in these parts could find herself in all kinds of trouble. I'll escort you back and, in future, perhaps you will see that you are accompanied at all times when leaving the house.'

Hester regarded him steadily without speaking, finding his manner somewhat forced. He was trying too hard to be friendly, she reflected, and was again struck by the sound of his voice.

She recalled the voices she had heard the evening before from the time of the coach hold-up to the moment she reached Tregowarth, and then it came to her like a bolt of lightning. Willard was the highwayman who had been at the head of the coach team during the hold-up.

'What ails thee?' Willard demanded. 'You look as if you have just seen a ghost.'

'Not a ghost,' Hester replied. 'I've been trying to puzzle out where I heard your voice before, and it has just come to me. You're Jack Savage, the highwayman!'

Willard's expression changed. His smile vanished and he lunged forward and grasped Hester by the shoulders to shake her violently. His powerful hands snaked up to her neck and tightened convulsively around the soft flesh.

'I suspected you would recognise me,' he ground out between glinting teeth. 'I had forgotten you might have been aboard that particular coach. This is an unfortunate business, Hester, because I have no option now but to get rid of you. Shall I fling you over the cliff to shut your mouth?' He paused and regarded her with cruel eyes. 'This is a pretty pass! Rufus has his daughter home at last, and I am forced to kill her.'

'I shall remain silent about this if you remove your hand,' Hester gasped.

Willard released her, his eyes narrowing as he considered, and Hester realised her life was balanced as if on a knife-edge. Then he shook his head, and his eyes glinted as he took in her fear, gleaming sadistically.

'I cannot trust you to remain silent,' he decided. 'And I cannot live with the knowledge that you have only to open your mouth to put me on the gallows. It is dangerous knowledge that you possess, and I see no other way around this problem but to kill you.'

'Does my father know who you really are?' Hester demanded.

Willard laughed. 'Not at all. I have everyone fooled; except you, it seems.'

'I swear not to tell a soul,' Hester clasped her hands together to still their trembling. 'My lips are sealed.'

'Talk is cheap!' He shook his head. 'You would promise me anything at this moment to save your neck, and then squawk like a wet hen the minute you are out of my company. I cannot trust you.'

He grasped Hester and began pushing her towards the sheer drop of the cliff. Hester tried to stop their progress but he was much too strong for her. They reached the very edge of the cliff, and Hester could feel the almost magnetic pull of the long drop through space to the rough surface of the sea beating against the rocks. Her senses spun sickeningly as she tried to resist the power of his strong arms.

'Please!' she gasped. 'Don't kill me!'

Willard looked down from his greater height. His face was like a mask of the Devil, his eyes narrowed and filled with deadly intention.

'How can I trust you?' he queried. 'My life depends upon my secrecy. I see no alternative.'

A voice called echoingly, and they both turned their heads in the direction from whence it came. Hester saw a rider coming along the cliff top from the direction of Polgarron and recognised Hal Trevian, mounted on a powerful bay and leading the horse he had borrowed from Rufus the night before.

Relief swamped her as Willard led her back a few steps from the precipice and released her. He was smiling now, but his expression was cruel.

'I'll kill Trevian if I have to,' he said fiercely. 'Taking life means nothing to me. I'll accept you at your word for now, Hester. Keep your lips sealed about me and I'll let you live. But I shall be watching you very carefully in future.'

Hester gasped in relief. Willard moved away to where his horse was cropping the thick grass and swung into the saddle. He rode back to Tregowarth as Hal Trevian arrived.

'Good morning, Hester,' Hal called cheerfully. 'I expected you to be abed at least until noon after your adventures last night. Are you quite recovered from your ordeal?'

He dismounted but retained his hold on the reins of both horses, and smiled at Hester, his handsome face showing pleasure at seeing her. He glanced in the direction Willard had taken, and his smile faded momentarily.

'You and Willard were standing dangerously close to the cliff edge,' he observed, 'and Willard should know better than to risk you like that.'

'It was quite safe,' Hester replied. 'I had walked too far from the house and Rufus sent Willard to fetch me back for breakfast.'

'Can you ride?' Hal offered.

'Yes. Mother felt that I should have some accomplishments, and riding was one of them.'

Hal trailed the reins of his own horse and came around the other animal to help Hester into the saddle. Her long dress proved to be something of a hindrance until she lifted it to her knees, and Hal settled her into the saddle and handed over the reins.

'He's a quiet horse,' he remarked,

regaining his own saddle, 'but be sure to keep him away from the cliff edge.'

Hester put her heels into the animal's flanks and set off at a trot, and Hal quickly joined her. 'You ride well,' he observed.

'I'm accustomed to a side saddle,' she retorted, and pushed the horse into a gallop. The pounding of hooves echoed the fast beating of her heart, and she felt exhilarated after the fear Willard had generated in her. She could see Willard in the distance, and wondered what she should do about him. That he would kill her if she broke her word to him she did not doubt.

Dare she confide in Hal? She glanced at him, and he smiled, meeting her gaze, and she realised that she would merely be placing his life in danger by taking him into her confidence, and the same problem would exist if she spoke of the situation to her father.

They quickly reached the house. Willard was standing at the top of the terrace steps with Rufus when she and

Hal reined in at the bottom. Hester slid out of the saddle as Rufus descended the steps towards them.

'You're an early bird, Hester, just like your mother,' he declared. 'But please don't leave the house alone in future. Always take one of the stable lads with you if you want to saunter along the cliffs. These are bad times for a wench to be out alone. Come and have breakfast.

'I plan to take you into Polgarron today and show you around. You must come in, Trevian, and have breakfast with us. I'm thinking you can introduce Hester to the kind of people in your circle of friends that she should meet.'

'I'll be pleased to,' Hal replied. 'But I cannot stay for breakfast. I have to be in court in Polgarron early this morning, and must return there immediately.'

'Very well.' Rufus took Hester's arm and turned to ascend the steps to the terrace. 'Feel free to call at any time.'

Hester glanced back when they reached the top step and saw Hal riding back the way they had come. He twisted in his saddle and waved before continuing steadily.

'You could do much worse than gain an interest in Hal Trevian,' Rufus observed as they entered the house. 'He inherited his father's law business, and has handled Tregowarth affairs ever since. What do you think of our Cornish scenery?'

'It is fascinating, and I cannot wait to explore further.'

Edmund was waiting just inside the house, a hand on the door as if impatient to close it. His keen gaze seemed to bite into Hester as she passed him, but his eyes were focused into the distance, gazing along the avenue that led to the house.

'A rider is approaching,' he observed.

Rufus swung round quickly and peered in the direction indicated. 'Who the Devil can be calling at this time of the morning?' he remarked irritably.

'It looks like Alan Grieve,' Edmund

replied. 'I'd know his piebald any-where.'

'One of Willard's friends,' Rufus growled. 'Tell Willard that Grieve is on the point of arriving, Edmund, and inform him that I do not want that man in the house at this time of the morning. In fact, I'd be happy if Grieve never darkened the doorstep again. He's involved in shady activities.'

Edmund closed the front door and hurried across the hall to knock at a door before opening it. Hester heard the sound of muttered voices, and then Willard appeared and crossed to the entrance. He went outside quickly, and Hester wondered if his friends were also involved in the nefarious business of robbing coaches.

Rufus took Hester's arm to lead her along the passage and into the dining room, where Agatha was waiting with a maid in attendance. Several dishes were standing on a sideboard, and Agatha turned to serve breakfast.

Hester gazed at her father's impassive

face, and he reached out a great paw of a hand, grasped her wrist, and drew her close to him.

'You must tell me if you suffer any slight at the hands of anyone who comes to this house, Hester,' he said earnestly. 'I will not have you troubled by any of the bad characters who show up here occasionally. I mean to keep a close eye on you, and it would make me very happy if you discovered a suitable man quickly and found refuge in wedlock.'

'Marry in haste, repent at leisure,' Hester quoted, and Rufus laughed.

'Let us partake of breakfast,' he said. 'Afterwards, you can dress for Polgarron and we'll take the carriage there.'

'My clothes were on the coach last night,' Hester observed. 'All I have is what I stand up in.'

'I doubt if Jack Savage would steal a lady's clothes.' Rufus laughed. 'I expect your luggage will turn up in a few days. Perhaps you can borrow something from Agatha to be going on with. She may be old, but she is still a woman.'

'Her ideas of style will differ greatly from mine, Father,' Hester rebuked.

'Then we shall shop in Polgarron first thing and get what you need.' Rufus sat down at the table. 'Come along, Agatha, don't keep us waiting for vittles.'

Willard appeared and sat down at the table. He helped himself to food and began to eat quickly. Hester kept her eyes lowered, not wanting to meet Willard's gaze, and an uncomfortable silence seemed to grasp her by the throat. Rufus ate noisily, unaware of any byplay at the table, and looked up at Willard eventually.

'What did Grieve want at this hour?' he demanded.

'He came to tell me that Andy Petch was discovered lying dead on the Polgarron road this morning, killed by a pistol ball. It seems he was one of the two men who attempted to rob the Plymouth coach last night.'

'And Grieve rode out from Polgarron

at this unearthly hour to inform you, did he?' Rufus demanded. 'Why should he think you would be interested in Petch?'

'Andy was a friend,' Willard replied sharply.

'And did you know he was involved in robbing coaches?'

'Of course not! Grieve also wanted to inform us that Hester's luggage is safe in Polgarron. Jack Savage chased the coach almost into town last night, and was deterred finally by a chance shot from the driver, who says he wounded Savage.'

'It's about time Savage was caught,' Rufus declared. 'I don't like any of your friends, Willard, as I've told you many times. A man is known by the company he keeps, and you seem to have fallen in with a circle of ne'er-do-wells.'

'I'm not responsible for what they do,' Willard retorted, his cold gaze on Hester's pale features, and she saw grim humour in his gaze. 'I do my work well here on the estate, and that's all you should be concerned with. I never listen to gossip about other people, and I won't have my own life talked about. I come and go as I please, and more than that you cannot expect.'

'I don't expect anything,' Rufus replied, shaking his head. 'All I ask is that you stay out of the way of temptation and live a good life. I pulled you out of the sea when you were a boy, and I'll throw you back the moment you slip from the straight and narrow path.'

Willard's dark gaze sought out Hester's eyes again and held her attention against her will. She squirmed in her seat and her heartbeats quickened when she saw deadly intention in his eyes.

'I have never done anything I should be ashamed of,' Willard said softly, 'and I would fight to the death against anyone to prove it.'

Hester sat with downcast eyes, frightened by the intensity in Willard's voice. She knew he was living a great lie, but dared not even consider revealing her deadly knowledge, and could only view her immediate future with great trepidation.

4

Despite her fears for the future, Hester soon discovered that life was indeed quite interesting as the days of the ensuing week passed, despite the uncertainty of Willard's presence and implied threat to her happiness. But Hal was never far away during her settling-in period. He arrived at Tregowarth with her missing luggage, and then called at various times every day to visit her. Hester was always pleased to see him. It was as if a bond existed between them from the outset, its links forged by the adventure of their initial meeting.

Hal took her riding along the cliffs to show her the sights, and as the days passed Hester found great relief in his company. It was easy to be friends with a man like Hal.

He was attentive and selfless, ready

with a smile or good advice, and by the time a week passed, Hester was aware in her heart that she would miss his company terribly if he suddenly stopped his visits.

Rufus remarked on the growing situation. 'I suspect you are taking my advice about finding yourself a husband and settling down,' he observed after Hal had departed from an afternoon visit.

'I like Hal,' Hester replied. 'He saved my life, and I am eternally thankful to him.'

'Well you could do much worse than marry him,' Rufus growled.

'You sound as if you want to be rid of me after I've spent only a week in your house,' Hester observed.

'Now don't go thinking like that.' Rufus shook his head. 'Truth to tell, I am worried about you. You're my daughter, and I have no idea how to handle that. I'm afraid I might do or say the wrong thing, so I'd rather see you married and contented with a husband than run the risk of doing something wrong.'

'It's wrong to be talking up a husband for me,' Hester told him.

Rufus laughed. 'Very well, I shall remain dumb on that subject in future.'

Hester nodded, but her father's talk of marriage stuck in her mind and she considered Hal and what he had come to mean to her. She liked him considerably, she was aware, but could she love him?

Willard was apparently not happy with the developing situation that he saw as being dangerous to his peace of mind. He waylaid Hester around the house, always with the same topic of conversation uppermost in his thoughts.

'Have you considered that the threat to your life could be removed completely if you married me?' he demanded when he confronted her in the library.

'Marry you?' Hester regarded him with narrowed gaze and a bleak expression. 'I have no feelings whatever for you, Willard. I'm appalled by what you have done as Jack Savage. You've murdered people in cold blood. You are living a lie in this house, and you care not what would happen to my father if he learned the truth about you. No, Willard, marrying you would never be an option. I think I would rather be dead than contemplate such a solution to my problem.'

'That eventuality can easily be arranged,' he retorted harshly.

Rufus entered the library and Willard departed.

'How are you getting along with Willard?' Rufus enquired. 'When I first heard that you would come to live here I entertained a hope that you might fall in love with Willard and marry him, but I can see now that the wind is blowing in a totally opposite direction. It is Hal who is uppermost in your mind.' He held up a hand as Hester began to protest. 'Now, I'm not sticking my nose in again. I want to take you into Polgarron tomorrow, so be ready to leave about ten in the morning.'

When breakfast was finished the next morning, Hester prepared for the trip to Polgarron. Promptly at ten, Rufus escorted her to the family coach drawn up at the bottom of the entrance steps, and Hester drew back in dismay as she was about to enter the coach, for Willard was seated inside, but he ignored her beyond a harsh greeting, and she sat down beside him while Rufus occupied the opposite seat.

Hester felt uncomfortable in Willard's presence, and made much of the passing scenery as they followed the coast road to Polgarron. Rufus spoke mostly to Willard, discussing estate business, and Hester was relieved that they did not attempt to draw her into their conversation. The coach passed along the cliffs hemming in several small coves and, when they reached the headland overlooking Polgarron Bay, Rufus called to the coachman to halt.

Rufus alighted and helped Hester from the vehicle, and she was delighted by the view as she looked across the bay to where Polgarron was clustered on the opposite headland above a stone harbour that jutted out into the glistening sea. Small houses littered the slopes as if they had been flung down by a capricious giant hand.

'You've been here a week and haven't seen the tower yet,' Rufus observed.

'What a beautiful view!' Hester exclaimed. 'It is so charming with the sun highlighting everything from that direction.'

'Let's go and you can view the town from close up.' Rufus uttered a wry laugh. 'You may not like it so much when you smell the fish, and the mud at low tide.'

'Do you know any smugglers, Father?' Hester asked as they re-entered the coach.

Rufus glanced sideways at her as he sat down in the opposite corner, and she was aware that Willard was watching her closely. The coach went on, and Rufus shook his head, his pale eyes narrowed as he regarded her silently for some moments.

'I expect your head is filled with romantic notions of the smuggling business,' he observed at length. 'You should not believe all you read about the poor devils who are forced by circumstance to follow that dangerous way of life. Smugglers don't risk their lives for the fun of it, Hester. Just consider that it may be the only way they can make a living.'

'I have read that smugglers pit themselves against the authorities to bring brandy, tea and other commodities unlawfully into the country because taxes are far too high,' Hester observed.

'And that's only the half of it.' Rufus glanced out across the bay, his expression harsh. 'The only commodity around here worth exporting is wool, and the government taxes that to high heaven. So it is two-way traffic across the Channel. The French take wool in payment for their goods. You'd better hope that you never find yourself in a position of witnessing smugglers at work,' he added softly. 'They would kill you out of hand to preserve their secrecy. You had a very narrow escape on the night of your arrival.'

Polgarron was a community lying in a low area of ground in a valley between high cliffs where a narrow river flowed into the sea. Houses and cottages were clustered around the stone quay and the waterfront, where stacks of lobster pots and drying fishing nets were evident everywhere.

Small boats occupied all available space along the quay and jetties, and Hester had her first smell of stale fish as Rufus helped her from the coach in front of the Fisherman's Arms; a sprawling, two-storey tavern with dusty windows overlooking the bay. Willard alighted and departed, calling a brusque farewell to Rufus and bestowing a glowering glance in Hester's direction.

Rufus took Hester's arm and led her into the tavern, having to duck his head to pass through the low doorway.

'Amos, where are you?' he called from the gloomy threshold, and his

68

loud voice echoed in the dusty corners of the long room.

A short, fat man wearing a dingy white apron appeared in a doorway behind the bar, and stood looking at them while he wiped his hands on a grey cloth. His dark hair was tousled, his fleshy face tanned. His brown eyes were alerted and quick, like a bird's, and his pointed chin jutted aggressively as he nodded a greeting.

'Morning, Rufus.' His voice was hoarse and rasping. 'I've been expecting you all week. 'Twas a bad business when Frank Stubbs brought the coach in like the Devil was chasing him. Fair put out, he was, an' all. Claimed Jack Savage had chased him the last eight miles to town, shooting pistol balls into the back of the coach because he wouldn't stop. I sent Barney Willgrass to check where the hold-up took place, and he came back with two bodies — Andy Petch and the coach guard, Tom Baldwin.

'Frank said Baldwin shot one of the

69

robbers and Savage shot Baldwin; and Barney found Petch lying out there with Baldwin — both dead; so it's obvious Petch was one of the two robbers who stopped the coach.'

'So who is Jack Savage?' Rufus demanded. 'It should be easy to work that out by going over Petch's friends. Petch always hung out with a bunch of ne'er-do-wells.'

Hester fought against the urge to declare what she knew about Willard, but her throat was dry and she kept her lips compressed.

'So this is your daughter, eh?' Amos Redfern observed. 'You had a narrow escape, by all accounts. It was lucky Hal Trevian was afoot and on hand to aid you. Did you see anything of the smugglers?'

'No.' Hester shook her head. 'And I didn't get a chance to see what Jack Savage looked like either.'

'Jethro Scarfe has been around, asking questions,' Redfern mused, 'but he ain't got enough sense to cover his thumb nail with. It's time the town found another watchman. Scarfe is useless, and I wonder why he got that job in the first place.'

Rufus laughed. 'Didn't they pick him because they knew he wouldn't be able to track down smugglers and highwaymen?'

'There's that to it,' Amos rumbled. 'At the moment he's running around like a chicken with its head cut off. He'll be coming out to Tregowarth to talk to Miss Hendry when he can get around to it, but don't expect him to solve anything or make any arrests.'

'I'm going to introduce Hester to Polgarron, and I'm hoping she will like it enough to want to stay here,' Rufus said. 'After her experience when she arrived, I wouldn't be surprised if she got on the next coach and went back to London.'

'She was born at Tregowarth, wasn't she?' Redfern showed broken and blackened teeth in a crooked smile at Hester. 'She's got Cornish blood in her, Rufus, and she answered the call of that blood by coming here — and by the look of her I'd say she ain't easily scared by anything.'

Rufus led Hester out to the street and paused to look around. Hester was eager to explore the narrow cobbled streets, and was somewhat relieved when a man approached Rufus and talked of having urgent business. Rufus immediately suggested that she should look around on her own.

'You'll get on so much better alone,' he pointed out. 'Traipsing around with me would bore you to tears.' He produced a small leather bag which clinked metallically when he offered it to Hester. 'Here's some money. Go and buy whatever takes your fancy. I'll see you back here at the tavern at noon. You should be all right on your own. Just tell everyone you meet that you're Rufus Hendry's daughter from London, and no-one will dare harm you.'

Hester took the money and looked around as Rufus moved away. She watched him cross the narrow street and enter an office before walking in the opposite direction, feeling the need to find solitude in which to contemplate the situation. Thoughts of Willard were weighing heavily upon her mind, and she kept an alert eye on her surroundings as she took in her first sight of Polgarron with its narrow, cobble-stoned streets.

She left the waterfront to look in several shops, picking her way over uneven cobblestones, and was peering through a dusty shop window when a man bumped into her, apparently accidentally, and apologised profusely as he backed away. He had disappeared into a nearby alley by the time Hester discovered that she no longer had the bag of coins Rufus had given her.

She stood stock-still in shock. The man had stolen her money, and she was aghast at his audacious slickness. She went to the mouth of the alley but it was now deserted, and she gazed around in disbelief. She had been robbed!

She chanced to see a brass plate beside a nearby office door, and relief filled her when she saw Hal Trevian's name upon it. She entered the office to find an older man, writing steadily in a thick ledger, seated at a high desk before a tall window.

'Good morning, Miss. Can I help you?' he asked, putting down his quill.

'I'd like to see Hal Trevian.' Hester replied.

'Do you have an appointment, Miss?'

'I'm afraid I don't, but I must see Hal, and it is urgent. I'm sure he will want to see me.'

'One moment, and I'll check if he is able to see you. Who shall I say is calling?'

'Hester Hendry.' She used her father's name as if it were a magic password.

The man's face changed expression as he slid off his stood and crossed to an inner door. Hester drew a deep breath and tried to control the fast beating of her heart. She was badly shocked by what had occurred, and wished she had not wandered off alone. In view of Willard's threats, she should have been more careful.

Hal Trevian emerged from his office and came to her side, smiling a greeting, his dark eyes sparkling with pleasure. Hester regarded him as if she had never seen him before, although her heart warmed at the sight of him. She gazed critically at him, aware that her impression was one of distinct approval.

He was not overly tall but of broad and powerful build. His smooth face was tanned, his features quite handsome, and she realised that she felt a sense of rapport with him because they had shared danger on the night of her arrival, and she could still recall the strength of his arms when he had held her.

'Hester, this is a pleasant surprise.' Hal grasped her hand and raised her fingers to her lips. 'I have just returned from the court. Are you alone in town?'

'Father brought me in, and then left me because of business. I'm so sorry to trouble you, Hal, but I've just been robbed.'

She explained what had occurred, and Hal shook his head.

'You should have been warned against the blackguards who infest our streets,' he said. 'Did you get a good look at the robber?'

'Not really! He was so good at robbing me that I didn't miss the money until he had gone. He was a short man, stocky, with a hat pulled low over his eyes, and he disappeared into an alley so quickly I had to wonder whether I really saw him at all. I'm sure he had a small gold earring in his left ear,' she added as an afterthought, 'and I think I should know him again if I saw him.'

'That description covers at least half the men of Polgarron.' Hal shook his head.

'And you were sight-seeing on your own. What was Rufus thinking about, letting you out alone? May I offer you my company for the morning? The case I was handling in court came to an unexpectedly swift end when my client changed his plea to guilty, so now I am free, and I should welcome the opportunity to attend you. We might be able to get a look at the robber.'

Hester regarded him with a gaze that was filled with pleasure and she nodded eagerly.

'Thank you, Hal,' she replied happily. 'But I shall accept your kind offer only if you assure me that I shall not be taking you away from your work. I seem to have gotten off on the wrong foot in Cornwall, and I feel that I need to break this procession of bad events. But you have been very good, and you've already given up a great amount of your time showing me around. Are you sure I am not imposing on you?'

'I have no appointments until this afternoon, and should be happy to accompany you,' he responded. 'Per- haps I can show you a better facet of life in Polgarron. There is one, I can assure you.'

Hester accepted happily, and Hal fetched his hat and escorted her from the office.

'There is one fashionable coffee house in town,' he explained, 'and it is certainly the place to be seen in. It's a little early in the day to meet those people I wish to introduce to you, but it will be as well for you to be seen as a friend of mine.'

Hester felt comfortable in Hal's company, and walked with her hand resting on his arm. He pointed out places of interest and gave a commentary on them as they passed. They entered an imposing building that turned out to be the fashionable coffee shop, and sat at a window table where Hester could watch the passers-by on the street while they drank coffee.

There were about a dozen men in the shop, and six of them were seated around a large centre table, playing cards. Looking around, Hester was dismayed to see Willard numbered among those at the card table, and his dark gaze lifted to her face.

'I am giving a ball next Saturday evening,' Hal said, 'and you shall be my guest of honour, which will afford me the opportunity to introduce you to my friends. There are a number of young women of your age who will prove good company for you if you so wish. They are girls you would have grown up with had you not been taken to London. We must endeavour to get you to pick up the threads of life here in Cornwall as soon as possible.'

'You're very kind.' Hester smiled. 'I didn't have many friends in London — mother disapproved of them, and I am so looking forward to changing my life completely.'

'We shall effect some changes.' Hal nodded. 'There isn't much to do in Polgarron, but we spare no efforts to keep boredom at bay.' He glanced around the big room. 'I see Willard has lost no time in getting into the game that runs non-stop here. Men join in and drop out, but the game continues all day, and sometimes right through the night.'

'I thought Willard was running the Hendry estate,' Hester observed.

'He has a good steward looking after the estate, which gives him an unlimited amount of free time. I've noticed that Rufus is rather indulgent where Willard is concerned. Willard can do no wrong. They frequently go to London on extended visits, gambling and the like.'

Hester watched Willard for some minutes, and presently a man arrived and crossed to the card table to slip into an empty seat beside Willard. Hester stiffened as she studied the newcomer, and shock spilled through her when she recognised him as the man who had robbed her. She suppressed a gasp, and Hal glanced at her.

'Is something amiss?' he enquired. 'You have turned quite pale.'

'The man who just came in and is

sitting on Willard's right looks like the man who robbed me.'

'What? Are you certain? That's Jeremy Suffling, who owns two fishing boats and a fish-curing house. I think you may be mistaken, Hester. He is an honest businessman who would hardly resort to stealing.'

'I'm certain he is the man who robbed me,' Hester insisted.

'Then we shall accost him and ask him to account for his recent movements.'

Hal started to his feet but Hester grasped his arm, restraining his movement. 'I don't think that would be wise,' she observed.

'But if he is the man who robbed you then he should have your money in his possession.

'And if he is going to gamble he may use my money to do so, and will have to produce the little bag the money was in.'

'Can you describe the bag? Would you know it if you saw it again?'

'Rufus certainly would.' Hester's gaze was sharp and bright. 'It belongs to him.'

'Then let us watch, although I cannot believe Suffling has become a common thief. I handle his business accounts, and I know he has no financial problems.'

'Perhaps he has another reason for robbing me.'

Hal regarded her with shock in his dark eyes.

'What makes you say that? Suffling is a particular friend of Willard. Is there some connection between them?'

'Let us watch and find out,' Hester countered.

Suffling said something to Willard, whose gaze lifted in Hester's direction, and then Suffling reached into an inside pocket and produced a small brown soft leather money bag. Hester suppressed a gasp, for she could plainly see the embroidered letters RH on the side of the bag, which she had noticed when Rufus gave it to her. She was further surprised when Suffling handed the bag to Willard before arising to leave.

'Stay, Jeremy,' Hal called as Suffling went to the door. 'I need to talk to you.'

Hester gulped at the lump which came to her throat as her tension flared. Her heart seemed to accelerate its beating and she felt stifled with nervousness as Hal arose and went forward, afraid that she had started something that might get badly out of control . . .

5

Silence fell upon the big room as Hal arose and went forward to the large table. The card players were frozen in their actions and gazed fixedly at his approach. Willard's face slipped into a guarded smile, but his dark eyes gleamed with stirring emotion as he regarded Hester, who stiffened in horror as she watched as if experiencing a bad dream.

'Willard, that leather money bag you are holding belongs to Rufus, who gave it to Hester this morning,' Hal challenged. 'How is it that Jeremy just handed it to you?'

Willard glanced down at the bag in question, hefting it in his hand as his smile widened. He glanced at Suffling, who had halted at the door.

'How did you come by this, Jeremy?' Willard enquired.

'I found it in the street a few minutes ago,' Suffling replied. 'I recognised it as belonging to Rufus and brought it here. No doubt you will return it to Rufus, Willard.'

'It was stolen from my pocket,' Hester said firmly, her gaze fixed on Suffling's face. 'It was done very neatly, but I felt its weight leave me, and by the time I realised what had happened you, sir, were disappearing into an alley. I recognise you quite easily. You brushed against me, and I felt you lift the bag.'

'You mistake me for someone else, mistress.' Suffling came slowly back to the table, his face alive with conflicting expressions. 'Did you not see me return the bag to Willard?'

'That does not prove anything,' Hal cut in. 'Miss Hendry recognises you without doubt, Jeremy, so you had better give us the truth of the event.'

'I suspect some cut-purse was responsible, dropped the bag in escaping, and I found it, and, as you saw, returned it to Willard. What more is a man to do? I did not know Rufus had given the money to his daughter, or that he had a daughter, come to that, else I should have returned it to her without bothering Willard.'

The bag clinked metallically on the table as Willard tossed it in Hester's direction.

'Take it, Hester,' he directed, 'and be more careful in future. It was lucky Jeremy found it or you wouldn't have seen it again. Thank you, Jeremy, for your honesty. There are many in town would have pocketed it and said nothing.'

Hal picked up the bag and handed it to Hester, who slipped it into her pocket. Suffling turned and departed, closing the door loudly. Willard returned his attention to his cards, and moments later the interrupted game was resumed.

Hester glanced at Hal's face and saw a grim expression showing there. She wondered if he was angry, but he smiled as he returned her to their table.

'This is a pretty kettle of fish,' he

observed. 'What do you think lies behind it?'

'Do you doubt my word?' Hester enquired.

'Certainly not! I believe you implicitly. But I am intrigued by the puzzle they have set. Why on earth would Jeremy rob you and then return the money to Willard? Perhaps he did not realise you are a Hendry until he learned your identity here. I tell you, there are not many thieves in town who would willingly rob Rufus Hendry or his family. Perhaps Jeremy got cold feet when he saw Rufus's initials on the bag.'

'I expect that is the answer,' Hester agreed.

'And yet there is a shadow in your eyes,' Hal continued, gazing frowningly at her. 'I sense something is amiss, and I'd give a lot to know what it is. When I saw you and Willard on the cliff the morning I returned the horse I borrowed he seemed to be menacing you. Did something happen between you two? I know Willard is a strange man with an ungovernable temper when he is aroused. Is he afraid your appearance means his hopes of inheriting the Hendry estate on Rufus's death have evaporated? Was he threatening you that morning on the cliff, Hester?'

She shook her head. 'No, it was nothing like that. In fact, he was rather pleasant; offering to help me settle in, and spoke of introducing me to his friends. He couldn't have been nicer.'

Hal regarded her intently for some moments while Hester strove to remain unconcerned. He shook his head, and she warmed to him because of his apparent concern for her. He sighed and glanced around.

'If you won't tell me what is going on then I shall have to guess,' he said finally. 'But I want you to know that you can confide in me, Hester, and anything you care to tell me will go no further than my ears.'

'Thank you.' She forced a smile. 'I appreciate your offer, and will avail myself of it should I ever need help.'

'Would you like to continue shopping?' he suggested. 'I'm quite good at carrying packages, and I have an eye for fashion so my advice could be invaluable.' He placed a hand over hers. 'I do hope you will come to regard me as a good friend because I rather think you might have need of one.'

'You saved my life the night we met, and at some considerable risk to your own,' Hester replied, 'so I do regard you as a very good friend indeed. For my part, I hope I don't appear to be unfriendly because I've denied your help when you can obviously see something is wrong, and I hope you will continue to call on me to further our friendship.'

'I am quite concerned about you because I do foresee some difficulties arising in your life.'

'And doubtless coming from Willard's direction!' She glanced at Willard's intent face as he studied his cards, and recalled his threats. 'I admit that Willard is getting awkward.' She paused, trying to stop herself, but she felt as if a dam had breached in her mind and her flow of words burst out against her will. 'In fact, I don't really know which way to turn.'

She paused, wanting to change the subject, but blundered on, and felt much relief as she unburdened herself. 'Willard has made his position quite clear. He seems to be of a passionate nature, and I fear he may attempt to scare me into fleeing back to London, which perhaps is why Suffling accosted me.'

'So Willard was threatening you on the cliff that morning.' Hal's expression took on a bleakness that tightened his features. 'I sensed I was right about that. What did he say to you?'

'I'd rather not go into that now, but it was quite serious.'

'Perhaps you should talk to Rufus about it.'

'I think not. It may blow over if I remain silent.'

Hal shook his head. 'I'd like to know

what is afoot,' he said softly. 'I might be able to save you from a lot of trouble if I have an inkling of what is in Willard's mind.'

'He has asked me to marry him,' she admitted.

'And threatened you?' Hal's expression turned bleak as he gazed at Willard. 'I think he should be taught a sharp lesson. He is certainly in need of one.'

'Please don't do anything here,' Hester said worriedly. 'Leave it for now.'

'Ignoring Willard will not solve anything,' Hal responded, 'but I bow to your wishes. Let us depart from this establishment. What would you like to do now?'

'You could show me around the town.' Hester arose immediately, her heart fast-beating.

Hal took her arm and led her to the door. Hester struggled against the urge to take a final look at Willard's brooding face but failed, and glanced over her shoulder to see that he was watching her closely, his face set in grim lines and his eyes boring at her like gimlets. Hester stifled a cold shiver as they stepped out into the warm sunshine.

Hal chatted incessantly, imparting a mass of local information, and Hester realised that she liked the sound of his voice as well as his manner and appearance, and she experienced a sense of disappointment when they reached the Fisherman's Arms just before noon and entered to find Rufus seated at a corner table, drinking ale and apparently awaiting her arrival for lunch.

'I was thinking of raising a hue and cry for you, Hester,' Rufus observed when she seated herself at his table. His dark eyes were filled with a bullish expression that gave Hester some disquiet. 'I looked for you earlier, saw Willard in the coffee house, and learned from him what had befallen you. Are you sure it was Jeremy Suffling who lifted your money?'

'I really cannot swear to it,' Hester replied. 'All I can say is that I did not see anyone else around at the moment I was robbed.'

'I shall have a chat with Suffling when I see him,' Rufus promised. 'I'm glad you were on hand when Hester needed you, Trevian. I am doubly in your debt now.'

'I shall always be at Hester's service,' Hal replied stoutly, smiling when Hester looked up at him, but there were shadows in his eyes and a firm set to his mouth.

'There is someone I want you to meet, Hester.' Rufus turned his head and beckoned to a young man seated at an adjacent table. 'He's Thomas Tremain, only son of Sir William Tremain, the local Magistrate. Here you are, Tom. This is my daughter, Hester, just arrived from London. I hope you two will become fast friends. Hester doesn't know anybody in town at the moment, except Trevian, and, with your help, I have high hopes that she will quickly find her level in Polgarron and discover a whole circle of new friends.'

Hester's heart almost missed a beat at her father's words, and she gazed in some confusion at the newcomer, who seized hold of her hand and bowed over it. She caught a glimpse of Hal's face in the background — it had turned to stone at the sight of Tremain, and she instinctively suspected an ulterior motive behind her father's introduction. Rufus had plans to marry her off to this newcomer!

Thomas Tremain was tall and slim, dressed in very well-cut clothes and wearing a powdered wig and silver buckles on his shoes. His age was no more than twenty years. Under normal circumstances, Hester might have welcomed him as a future friend but, sensing what was in Rufus's mind, she rebelled against it with every fibre of her being.

'I am very happy to make your acquaintance, Miss Hendry,' Tremain said in a slightly high-pitched voice. 'It will give me great pleasure to know you, and I stand at your service. Perhaps I may call on you tomorrow morning at Tregowarth. You have recently come from London, I understand, and we ought to compare notes, for I do spend a great deal of time in the capital, and we may have some mutual friends there.'

'I think not,' Hester replied. 'I should think that you and I moved in rather different circles.'

'Come to Tregowarth at ten in the morning, Tom,' Rufus cut in. 'Hester will be awaiting you. Can you dine with us now?'

'Unfortunately not.' Tremain smiled and backed away, holding up a hand as if warding off an evil spirit. 'I have an appointment with my father which I cannot break. But I shall present myself at Tregowarth tomorrow morning without fail. I shall look forward to seeing you again, Miss Hendry.'

Hester thought it better to ignore the incident, but quickly realised that Rufus should be made aware of her feelings. She moistened her lips and drew a deep breath.

'That was rather obvious, Father,' she observed.

'What was?' Rufus smiled, but the expression in his eyes informed Hester that she had guessed rightly about his motives. 'You need friends to make your way in this county, and Tom Tremain has the highest credentials. He is a nice, upright young man, and you would be wise to cultivate his friendship. I'd be very pleased if you and he found some common ground on which to build a future together. Any father would welcome that eventuality.'

'I'm not accustomed to having a father's influence.' Hester met his gaze and held it, and Rufus saw accusation in her eyes and shook his head.

'That's why I'm trying to make up for lost time,' he countered. 'Don't be hard on me, Hester. I have much to learn about a father's relationship with a daughter. Just remember that I did not drive your mother away to London. She left me of her own accord. Did she ever tell you about our days together?'

'She spoke of you rarely, and I never once heard her say a good word about you.'

'So you see me as something of a tyrant!' Rufus smiled sadly. 'Very well, I shall endeavour to stay out of your business, unless I see you making an obvious mistake. Give young Tremain the cold shoulder when you see him tomorrow. I'll leave you in the hands of Hal here, and he will have to make the best of it. Why don't you stay and have a meal with us, Hal?'

'It would be my pleasure,' Hal replied. 'But I have an appointment early this afternoon, so I shall have to make haste.'

Hester was satisfied that she had stopped Rufus in his tracks, but she felt uneasy as the meal unfolded, and when Hal took his leave somewhat abruptly afterwards, apologising for his undue haste, she wondered if their future relationship would be discoloured by the advent of Tom Tremain in her life.

'I have some more business to conduct this afternoon,' Rufus said at length, 'but after your experience of this morning I hesitate to suggest that you should go off alone and explore the town, but I am sure you wouldn't want to accompany me and listen to a lot of boring business talk.'

'I shall be perfectly all right on my own,' Hester replied.

'I should have brought Agatha along this morning,' Rufus remarked. 'She is a good chaperone. She wouldn't let any stranger get within a mile of you.'

Hester smiled. 'I think I would rather not have Agatha as a companion. I'm perfectly capable of amusing myself, Father. I am on my guard now so I shall manage alone. Shall I meet you back here later?'

'Yes, say about four o'clock. If you do get back early you can go into a back room here and wait for me. Just come in and ask for Amos and he will take good care of you.'

Hester nodded and took her leave, her brow wrinkled by a frown. She wondered why her father had wanted her to come and live at Tregowarth, for it seemed that she might be something of an embarrassment to him, which was obviously how Willard saw her. She walked along the main street, but could summon up no enthusiasm for shopping, and found her steps leading to the waterfront.

The sky had darkened since the morning, and clouds, seemingly laden with rain, were scurrying overhead, chivvied by a strong gusting breeze. The open sea looked less inviting now, its surface marred by choppy waves that came running up the narrow beach in quick succession.

Hester found a seat by the mouth of an alley between two barn-like buildings that protected her from the rising wind. She was feeling unsettled, and considered her decision to come and live in Cornwall. Rufus did not seem entirely happy with her arrival, and she was afraid of Willard, whose dark, unfathomable eyes had seemed to boost her belief that he would stop at nothing to get whatever he wanted.

She pondered over the question of returning to London and resuming her life there. But she sensed that Willard would not permit her to escape. He could not accept that she would remain silent about him, and a shiver darted through her as she looked at the situation from his point of view.

She had been tempted several times during the past week to inform Rufus of what she had learned about Willard, but at this point in time she did not know if her father would protect her or side with Willard. Perhaps Rufus was in league with Willard!

Rain began to fall, and Hester stirred. She arose, moved back into the alley to a spot where the rain could not reach, and remained watching the changed scene of the little port.

The wind was rattling a loose board

in one of the buildings, slamming it monotonously without pause. The sound irritated Hester, but the rain was too heavy for her to move on. There had been more than a dozen men on the quay, some working on nets and lobster pots; others merely passing the time, but the inclement weather had driven them all under cover and the place was now eerily deserted.

A boot scraped a cobblestone behind Hester and she turned quickly, startled by the sound. Two men had emerged through a side door in the building where she was sheltering and were coming towards her. They were dressed as fishermen — wading boots and soiled smocks, and one cracked a joke which made the other laugh harshly. One fell behind the other to pass Hester and, when they were level with her, both whirled towards her, their calloused hands lifting to grasp her.

Hester opened her mouth to scream but a hand was clamped over her face. She was swept off her feet and carried back to the side door of the building. In a fleeting moment she had been removed as if spirited away, and the slamming door that cut her off from Polgarron sounded like the knell of doom in her shocked ears . . .

6

Hester tried to scream but the hand across her mouth almost prevented her breathing, and she knew the cool dread of despair as she was set upon her feet and held tightly by calloused hands. Her senses whirled in shock, and she feared she would faint as her heartbeats hammered and her pulses raced, but she was shaken roughly and the hand across her mouth was removed.

'Don't scream or it'll go bad with you,' one of the men said harshly.

'What do you want?' she gasped. 'Who are you?'

'That isn't for you to know.' The man holding Hester was tall and powerful, his weathered features coarse; his brown eyes narrowed and filled with a mean expression. He had a large, misshapen nose and hollow cheeks scarred by the ravages of smallpox. His strong hands grasped Hester's upper arms with a painful grip, and again he shook her roughly.

'What do you want?' Hester demanded. 'Did Willard send you?'

'Willard? Don't know any Willard,' the second man replied. He was smaller and older than his companion. 'Don't you know any better than to wander alone in this area? There are some around here would murder you just for the clothes you're wearing.'

'Is it money you want?' Hester managed to put her hand into her pocket, and her trembling fingers closed on the small bag of money Rufus had given her that morning. She produced the bag and held it out. The small man snatched it from her, opened it, and spilled its contents into a gnarled palm.

'We've struck it rich,' the big man gloated.

'You won't think you're lucky when my father learns of this,' Hester said.

'No-one is gonna learn anything about it. We'll cut your throat and drop you in the harbour. Dead folks don't tell tales.'

'Who is your father?' demanded the smaller man, putting the coins back in the bag. He saw the initials embroidered on the leather.

'Rufus Hendry.'

The small man muttered an unintelligible curse and almost dropped the bag in sudden agitation.

'Is your father Rufus Hendry?' he demanded, and swung round on his taller companion. 'Did you hear that, Barney? What kind of game is Willard playing? He's set us against Rufus.'

'Do you know my father?' Hester demanded.

'I don't like this one little bit.' The small man handed the money bag back to Hester. 'I ain't getting mixed up in this, Barney. We'll be up to our necks in bad trouble when Rufus misses his daughter. You better go back to Willard and find out what he's playing at, and tell him to find two other fools to do his dirty work.'

'Too late,' Barney replied. 'She knows what we look like. The minute we turn her loose she'll go straight to Rufus, and that'll cook our goose. We've gone too far now to pull out.'

'Well, you can do what you like,' the smaller man retorted, 'but I'm not having anything to do with this. I'm getting out of here, and you can remember, Miss, that I backed off soon as I learned who you are. This is the last time I work for Willard Cooper.'

Hester watched in growing surprise as the smaller man turned, hurried to the door, and departed. The magic of her father's name did not escape her notice. And she looked at her remaining captor, aware that his manner had changed. When the wind rattled the side door and it flew inwards he jumped like a startled rabbit, ran to the door, and slammed and bolted it as if Rufus was already bearing down upon him.

'Sit down on that keg,' he snarled, coming back to Hester. 'I ain't running.

I'll tie you and leave you while I go talk to Willard. No-one will find you in here, and you could shout all day and not be heard.'

'Let me go,' Hester suggested, 'and I'll not breathe a word about what happened. I know Willard is really Jack Savage, the highwayman, but I've stayed silent about him, and I won't talk about you either.'

'So that's why Willard wants you out of the way! How did you find out about him?'

'I was on the coach when he held it up, and recognised his voice when he spoke to me later.'

The man guffawed and slapped his thigh. 'So Willard got too clever at last. Well, you sit down, my pretty, and stay quiet. I won't be gone more than a few minutes.'

He grasped Hester's arm, led her to an upturned keg, and forced her to sit upon it. When he moved away she looked around for a way of escape, but he returned within a moment holding a length of tarred rope. He bound her arms before roping her ankles together and tying a loose end to a nearby post.

'Now you sit there quiet while I see Willard,' he said sharply.

He left her then, departing by the side door. Hester heard a key turn in the lock, and a tense silence followed. She strained against the rope, but it might have been a metal chain for all its flexibility and she ceased to struggle after a few moments and looked despairingly around the gloomy interior, aware that the rain had driven everyone into shelter, leaving the little quayside deserted and desolate.

Her worst fears were now realised. She had hoped Willard would trust her to remain silent about his secret, but was aware now that with his life depending on her silence he could not afford to take any chances.

The tarred rope was hard and unyielding, but when Hester examined her wrists she saw that it had knotted badly. There was a small loop beside the knot where dried tar had prevented it from tightening smoothly, hence the loop, and which might be induced to loosen still more and free the frayed end if she could only hook it over some protuberance and exert pressure on it.

She examined the nearby post, saw several large nails sticking out from it, and tottered to her feet to hop unsteadily towards it.

She raised her hands and hooked the small loop over a large, square-cut nail and used her body weight to apply pressure to the loop. The dried tar was uneven, sharp, and scratched her wrists as she tried desperately to loosen the obdurate knot. She kept her gaze on the side door, afraid that Barney would return before she could get free, for she knew what kind of an answer he would bring from Willard.

The pain in her wrists became intolerable, and Hester was on the point of desisting when she felt the knot give a little. She paused, drew a deep breath, and then renewed her struggles with even greater determination.

After what seemed an age the knot gave a little more and loosened sufficiently to enable her to slip her sore wrists out of her bonds. Uttering a prayer of relief, she divested herself of the rope and ran to the side door.

The door was locked, and she threw her weight against it several times to no avail before she looked around for other means of escape. A large window in the front wall of the building, overlooking the harbour, attracted her and she ran to it, fearing that her captor would reappear at any moment. There was an opener on the right side of the window, but it was nailed and refused to budge. She wasted precious moments struggling with it until common sense warned it would be useless to continue.

Several long planks leaning in a corner attracted her attention and she ran to them, snatched up a thick piece of timber, and returned to the window to thrust an end of the plank against the dusty glass. The tall pane finally gave way and shards of glass flew in all directions. Hester dropped the plank and fetched the keg, which she stood upon to gain height, and then stepped on the window sill before jumping outside.

She fell to her knees but did not hesitate. She sprang up and began to run along the quay, wanting to find the sanctuary of the Fisherman's Arms. She turned into a narrow alley and continued to run. Relief and shocked reaction combined to elevate her to a high state of nerves, and she fled as if a thousand devils were hard upon her heels.

She ran to the tavern and blundered in through the doorway. Two men were standing on the threshold and Hester collided with one, who grasped her as she staggered sideways and began to fall. His powerful arms saved her from further mishap but she struggled against his grasp in blind panic until he spoke sharply.

'Hester, what ails thee?' Rufus

demanded. 'Get a grip of yourself.'

Relief swamped Hester as she looked up into her father's grim face. He supported her as she gasped out details of her frightening experience, and then half-carried her to a nearby table and seated her.

'Just look at you,' he said. 'You look like you've been dragged through a hedge backwards. Your wrists are bleeding, and there are smears of tar all over your dress. Now calm down and give me some details. What did the two men look like?'

'What does it matter about the two men?' she demanded wildly. 'They mentioned Willard's name, and he is Jack Savage, the highwayman. I recognised his voice.'

Rufus obtained a glass of rum and held it to Hester's lips. The fiery liquid burned her throat, seeming to cut through the tissues of fear gripping her, and she relaxed and her breathing became steadier.

'I was certain they were going to kill

me,' she said faintly. 'If I hadn't mentioned your name I'm sure I would be floating lifeless in the harbour at this very moment. Willard threatened to kill me last week, Father, and those two men were acting on his orders.'

'Stay here, where you will be safe,' Rufus ordered. 'I'll find Willard and see what he has to say for himself. You called one of those men Barney, and from your description of him I think he must be Barney Kepple.' He raised his voice and called for the innkeeper. 'Amos, keep an eye on my daughter while I'm gone. Send a boy to fetch Hal Trevian, and tell Trevian to guard Hester with his life. I want to find her here, safe and sound, when I return.'

Rufus departed with his companion, and Hester drew a deep breath and tried to relax as the innkeeper picked up a large pistol from behind the bar and came to seat himself opposite her at the table. He placed the pistol on the table, its wicked-looking muzzle pointing towards the door, his right hand resting easily on the butt.

'You said Willard is Jack Savage,' Amos observed. 'Are you sure you're not mistaken?'

'Are you going to send someone to fetch Hal Trevian?' Hester countered.

Amos twisted in his chair, making it creak with his weight. 'Bill, come on out here,' he called, and a youth emerged from the room behind the bar. 'You know Hal Trevian, the lawyer. Go thee along to his office and fetch him. Tell him Miss Hendry is here and needs his support.'

The youth departed and Hester relaxed a little. She looked down at her tar-stained gown and lacerated wrists, and wondered if she had been enveloped by a nightmare. How would Rufus resolve the problem of Willard being Jack Savage? What would Willard do when he was confronted with the revelation that his sins had found him out? She suppressed a shudder and tried to close her mind to the awfulness of reality.

Minutes later, Hal came bustling into the tavern, his face a mask of concern as he approached the table where Hester was seated. Amos withdrew, but remained in the background, pistol in hand. Hal sat down. He grasped Hester's hands and examined her wrists while shaking his head, and she blurted out the truth about Willard. Hal's cool gaze assessed her degree of shock and he looked up at the innkeeper.

'Amos, get a carriage at once. Tell Rufus I am taking his daughter to my house, where my mother will care for her. Send your boy to Doctor Spencer with a message for him to call on me at home. Hester needs medical help; something to help her get over the shock of her ordeal.'

'What about Willard?' Amos demanded. 'She's accused him of being Jack Savage.'

'Never mind that now,' Hal rapped. 'Get a carriage at once.'

Hester felt comforted by Hal's presence. She propped her head in her hands her elbows resting on the table top, and tears of relief trickled down her cheeks. Hal placed a hand on her shoulder.

'I'll take you to my home,' he said soothingly. 'You'll be safe there, and you'll like my mother. Don't worry now. Everything will be right.'

Hester was aware of an uncanny trembling in her breast which she was powerless to overcome. She looked at her sore wrists through a veil of tears that shimmered in her eyes and her fright seemed to multiply by leaps and bounds. An eternity seemed to pass before a carriage arrived at the door, and when she attempted to stand her legs would not support her. She could not even rise from her seat and gazed helplessly up at Hal.

He lifted her easily from the chair and carried her out to the coach. Hester closed her eyes, comforted by his strong arms. She felt weak and vulnerable, and rested her head thankfully on his broad shoulder. He settled her in the coach and sat by her side, holding her hands, and Hester rolled almost lifelessly with the motion of the vehicle as it moved off over the cobblestones.

They were well clear of Polgarron before Hester felt able to sit up and take notice of her surroundings. The carriage was travelling along a coast road and the sea was on her right hand. She looked up into Hal's intent face and he smiled encouragingly. The expression in his eyes was one of deep concern which spilled over into his voice when he spoke.

'How are you feeling now?' he enquired. 'Your shock seems to be receding and colour is coming back to your cheeks. I wish now that I had taken the time to accompany you this afternoon, but I thought Rufus would stay with you.'

'I am feeling much better,' Hester sighed heavily. 'I must look a sight! My gown is ruined. Can I hope that life in Cornwall will improve after this business?'

'We shall see that nothing else befalls you,' he said firmly. 'From now on, you will be able to enjoy your life.'

'What will happen to Willard?'

'If they prove he is Jack Savage then he will hang for his misdeeds and good riddance to him. He has robbed many coaches in his time, and murdered a number of travellers.'

Hester shivered and closed her eyes, her mental images too terrible to contemplate. If they hanged Willard it would be as a result of her evidence, and she dreaded to think she might be responsible for a man's death, whatever his crimes.

'Try not to think about it,' Hal urged. 'Jack Savage deserves to die.'

The coach went on until it reached a gateway in a high hall and turned into a gravelled drive that curved beneath a copse of trees and then crossed open parkland to a grey-stone mansion standing on a high cliff overlooking Polgarron Bay. Hal helped Hester from the vehicle, dismissed the driver, and led her up a steep flight of steps to a large doorway.

'This was my father's house,' Hal explained, 'but, alas, he is no longer with us. He died two years ago. I live here with my mother, and I am sure she will welcome your company until you have recovered from your ordeal. It will be safer if you stay here until Willard is behind bars.'

'Do you think he might try to harm me?'

'Even if they place him in custody, he would, I fear, arrange for his associates in crime to attack you.'

Hester tried to still her whirling thoughts. Her head was aching and she felt quite ill, but Hal's presence comforted her and she was relieved when the door opened as they reached it and a butler appeared.

'Lambert, this is Miss Hester Hendry, who will be staying with us for a few days. While she is here as a guest you will be responsible for her safety. No-one but her father, Rufus Hendry, shall be permitted to approach her.'

'Very well, Master Hal.' The butler

was tall and powerful, and he nodded as he took stock of Hester's appearance. 'Mistress Trevian is in the library. Shall I announce you?'

'No.' Hal took Hester's arm and led her across the wide hall and opened a door on the left.

The room they entered was wide, spacious, with tall windows overlooking parkland. Book shelves lined the walls. A white-haired lady of middle-age, elegantly beautiful, was seated in an easy chair by a tall window.

'Mother, this is Rufus Hendry's daughter, Hester, and I've invited her to stay with us for a few days. I told you about her this morning and, since that trouble last week, she has found more of the same today. She is badly shocked by her latest experience, and I expect Doctor Spencer to call shortly and check on her condition.'

Mrs Trevian arose and held out her hands. 'You are very welcome, Hester,' she greeted. 'What a terrible introduction to Cornwall you've had!

No wonder you are looking shocked. What on earth has happened? Come and sit down, my dear, and try to relax. Hal, get us some tea, would you? So you are Rufus Hendry's daughter. You look very much like your mother as I remember her. Oh, your poor wrists! And there is tar on your gown.'

Hester was relieved to sit down, and Mrs Trevian fussed around her until Hal returned bearing a tray. He poured tea into three cups and handed one to Hester, who sipped the hot liquid thankfully and felt better for it. She listened to Hal explaining her experiences to Mrs Trevian, and could scarcely believe that she had undergone such an ordeal. But the tea dispelled the cold feeling in her breast and her nerves began to settle.

They talked until the butler appeared, followed by a short, stout man who was carrying a brown leather bag.

'Doctor Spencer,' Lambert announced.
'I heard a buzz of news as I was

leaving Polgarron,' Spencer said. 'It seems they have captured the highwayman, Jack Savage. What on earth is this world coming to? You're looking very well, Mistress Trevian. When I received the summons from Hal I suspected it was you who was indisposed.'

'I'm very well, thank you, Doctor,' Mrs Trevian replied. 'We'd like you to run your eye over this young lady. She is Hester Hendry.'

'You look as if you've been in a battle, my dear,' Spencer observed. 'What has befallen you?'

Hester did not enlighten him. She sat with her eyes closed.

The doctor examined her whilst Hal recounted details of the ordeal she had suffered, and Spencer tut-tutted.

'I find nothing seriously wrong,' he pronounced at length. 'Badly shaken up but no real harm done.'

Hal sat down beside Hester and talked generally, which greatly lessened her fears. Later, when the doorbell pealed insistently, Hester stared nervously and Hal sprang to his feet.

'I expect that will be Rufus,' he said, and hurried from the room.

Hester sat in mental turmoil until the door was reopened and Hal returned, accompanied by Rufus, who face showed signs of violence. Her father's left eye was badly swollen and there was a long scratch on his left cheek that had seeped blood. Hester gazed at him in consternation, her imagination casting her to fear the worst.

'You're hurt, Father!' she exclaimed.

'It is little enough to pay for the capture of Jack Savage,' he retorted. 'Willard freely admitted everything when I confronted him, but had no intention of surrendering. He fought hard, but I got him in the end, and he's lodged in the gaol in Quay Street. You won't have any more trouble from him, Hester. He'll get a rope around his neck for what he's done, and it'll be good riddance to his bad blood. To think I've been harbouring such a villain all these years! You should have told me about

Willard as soon as you realised who he was.'

Hester suppressed a shudder. At that moment she was very much inclined to tell her father that she wanted to return immediately to London, for the capture of Jack Savage did not relieve her mind, but added to the problems that had to be faced.

7

Rufus was pleased when Hal suggested that Hester remain for a few days, and agreed instantly. Hester noted that her father seemed inordinately relieved to have her off his hands as he prepared to leave.

'I had a feeling you would prefer to stay here,' he said, 'I'll have your clothes sent from Tregowarth. If there is anything you lack then buy it in Polgarron and put it on my account. My credit is good anywhere in the town. You'll take care of her, Trevian?'

'I shall, most certainly!' Hal nodded. His gaze was on Hester's pale face. 'I plan to take a week from my work in order to devote myself to Hester's service. You can rest assured that no harm shall come to her.'

Rufus departed, and Hester suppressed a little sigh of relief as the door closed behind her father, aware that she was greatly suspicious of him; afraid he was involved in some nefarious local business that prevented him from wanting a close relationship with his only daughter.

'I wouldn't worry too much about Rufus's attitude,' Hal said softly. 'I can see that you are troubled by it. But that is the kind of man he is. The responsibilities of marriage and family were never his strong point, and you will have to make excuses for him if you are to understand him at all.'

'I'm coming to that conclusion,' Hester replied, 'and I shall need time in which to come to terms with this new life of mine. I only hope my arrival in Cornwall is not piling unwarranted pressure on you, Hal. I expect there are not enough hours in a day for you to complete all you need to do, and now you have had me thrust upon you.'

'Don't give it a second thought,' he hastened to assure her. 'It seems fate has arranged our paths to entwine, and we can only follow the dictates of what is ordained. We are both powerless in the grip of events, so I am quite prepared to go along with whatever evolves, and count myself fortunate to be in a position to help a damsel in distress.'

'You're very kind, Hal. But there is a dark side to this situation that worries me. Willard is completely ruthless. Do you think I have reason to fear for my life?'

'I'm afraid the situation will be fraught with danger while Willard lives.' Hal shook his head as he considered. 'But we are well aware of what could happen so we shall take measures to protect you. I'm sure they will lose no time in bringing Willard to trial, and then execute him, and you won't be really safe until he is dead, so we shall take steps to protect you.'

Hester fell silent, her fears vibrant. She recalled the two men who had seized her on the quay, and realised that it would be a simple matter for desperate men to get at her, whatever measures were employed to keep her safe.

Hal rang for the butler and Lambert tapped at the door of the room and entered.

'Lambert, I shall want to talk to you later about guarding the house while Miss Hendry is with us. We may need to bring in a watchman for the dark hours.'

Lambert nodded and withdrew. Hal looked searchingly into Hester's face, noting her pallor and tension.

'Would you like to go to your room?' he suggested. 'I do think you should rest until tomorrow.'

Hester nodded. Her head was aching and she felt exhausted and low-spirited. She staggered when she arose, and Hal placed a comforting hand under her left elbow and assisted her. Hester was relieved when they had negotiated the flight of stairs, and Hal led her into a large bedroom that had a marvellous view of the cliff and the sea. Mrs

Trevian was waiting there, and she smiled at Hester's cry of delight in beholding her surroundings.

In retrospect her ordeal seemed so unreal! She frowned as she considered, and realised there was a worse travail to come. She would have to give evidence against Willard at the assizes, and that knowledge was cold and hard in her mind. She lay back on the bed and tried to relax, closing her eyes although fearing she would not be able to sleep with such an overburdened mind.

But she fell asleep despite her worry, and was surprised, when she awakened, to find the day had passed and twilight was pressing in against the tall window. A lamp was alight on a chest of drawers beside the bed, its dim glow comforting.

Arising, she crossed to the window and peered out. Gone was the enchanting scene of cliffs and sky. Night had closed in, and she shivered as she wondered what it might be hiding. Those brutal friends of Willard might now be out there, biding their time, awaiting an opportunity to prevent her giving evidence against the notorious highwayman.

The bedroom door opened, startling Hester, and she turned quickly to see a tall, thin girl entering.

'Hello, Miss. I'm Daisy, the maid. I've looked in on you several times to ensure that you are all right, and Master Hal himself came to check on you. Did you have a good sleep?'

'Yes, thank you, Daisy.' Hester was pleased to see the girl, whose smiling face and cheerful manner did much to reassure her. 'I didn't think I could sleep, considering my state of mind, but I feel much better now.'

'You've had a nasty shock,' Daisy's dark eyes were wide with interest. 'And Willard Cooper turned out to be Jack Savage! I always thought he was a rascal not to trusted, but when I heard what happened to you, and why, I just couldn't believe it. Did he rob the coach for money, or was he after you because he knew you were aboard?'

'I don't know the answer to that.' Hester shook her head. 'I only know I recognised his voice, and foolishly blurted it out to him. If I'd had the sense to remain silent he would not have suspected that I had learned his secret, and I should have been spared this ordeal.'

'You'll be quite safe under this roof, Miss. Master Hal won't let anything bad happen to you. And you being Rufus Hendry's daughter, I shouldn't think anyone would want to get on the wrong side of him. Is there anything I can get you? Master Hal is in his study, and he asked me to take you to him if you feel the need for company.'

Daisy showed her into a large, square room, where Hal was seated at a desk with a stack of paperwork before him. He arose quickly when Hester entered, and his face expressed concern as he came to her side.

'You look less harassed now,' he observed. 'I'm so glad you managed to sleep.'

Hester nodded. 'I am much refreshed,' she replied, 'but feel quite guilty at being forced upon you like this.'

'Think nothing of it.' He smiled. 'I've been intending to take a holiday from my business but could not find sufficient reason to do so, but now you are here I have made the decision to leave my partner to handle the pressures for a week. I shall look forward to being with you, and will feel better for the break, so we shall be killing two birds with one stone and you will be doing me a favour by remaining. You will have some protection and I shall get a holiday.'

'If you really don't mind my company then I shall try to forget my unfortunate start to life in Cornwall and make an effort to come to terms with the situation.'

'I suspect there will be some more unpleasantness for you.' Hal took her arm and led her to a window seat. 'You will have to identify Willard as being Jack Savage, and give evidence at his trial, but when you've done that you should be able to settle down to your new life. Jethro Scarfe, the watchman, came to talk to you earlier, but I would not let him disturb you, so he will return tomorrow to get a statement from you about the coach hold-up. Do you have a clear picture of that incident?'

Hester nodded. 'Every detail is burned into my mind. I recognised Willard's voice as belonging to Jack Savage when I heard him speak the morning after the coach was held up, and he threatened to kill me when I foolishly told him what I knew. If you had not come along when you did I'm certain he would have pushed me off the cliff.'

'It was unfortunate that you forewarned him of your suspicion, but we are prepared to defend you.' He glanced at his desk and Hester, following his gaze, suppressed a shiver when she saw a pistol lying there. 'Rufus went back to Polgarron to locate the two men who abducted you. He is sure he knows who they are, and if they are apprehended then there will be no immediate danger to you, although Willard has many friends who might want to help him escape justice.'

'And the only way he can do that is by having me silenced,' Hester observed.

Hal nodded. 'Fortunately, we are on our guard, so I shall be prepared if anything untoward develops. We are merely being careful, for with such a reputation, Jack Savage is not a man to take chances with. But enough of that subject. I want to help you forget what has happened. If you feel up to it, I should like to show you around the house.'

'Thank you.' Hester smiled. 'You have a very charming home.'

Hal was pleased by her reaction, and eagerly showed her around. Hester found her fears receding still further as they made a tour of the house with Hal explaining the many points of interest they came across. They ended up in the big kitchen, where Hal asked the house-keeper, Mrs Jenner, to prepare supper, and then he led Hester into a large drawing room and settled her at ease.

Hester realised that she was hungry, and ate the cold fare that was placed before her. Afterwards, they sat talking until Hester stifled a yawn, and Hal was observant enough to recognise the signs of tiredness in her.

'You have had more than your share of adventure today,' he said gently. 'I think it is time you retired. After Jethro Scarfe has taken a statement from you, I shall endeavour to interest you in less dramatic matters. You should be able to sleep comfortably tonight, for my room is next to yours and I shall be at your service if anything disturbs you.'

'Thank you. I shall be forever in your debt.'

'I consider it an honour to have you under my roof,' Hal replied softly.

He clasped her hands. Hester leaned towards him, drawn by some imponderable reaction, and kissed his cheek spontaneously. Hal paused and looked into her eyes, and then a long sigh escaped him and he took her slowly into his arms, prepared to stop if she protested. But Hester closed her eyes and pushed herself against him while he kissed her tenderly, their contact sending spasms of relief through Hester's taut body.

They remained close while time passed unmeasured, and when they drew apart Hester felt recharged by their contact. Her eyes were bright, almost feverish, and her breathing was ragged, as if she had been running.

'I'll see you in the morning.' Hal spoke huskily. He rang for Lambert, who appeared instantly, as if he had been waiting outside the door.

'Miss Hendry is going to her bedroom now, Lambert. Get Daisy to accompany her. We shall take a look around outside to check that no unauthorised persons are concealed in the shrubbery, and we shall remain alert for any move against the house.'

'I'm afraid I'm causing you a great deal of trouble,' Hester observed.

'Not at all.' Hal shook his head emphatically. You performed a great service to the community by denouncing Willard, and it is up to the rest of us now to do our bit by defending you against the reaction of the criminal element until the danger to yourself is removed.'

'Quite right, Miss.' Lambert nodded. 'We have to stand up to these desperate people or they would rule us as they pleased.'

Daisy was summoned, and the girl chattered in lively fashion as she accompanied Hester to her room.

'I shall be sleeping in your dressing room tonight,' Daisy informed Hester.

When she was finally in bed and ready to sleep she discovered that the fears vibrant in her breast combined to drive all thought of rest from her mind. She lay in the darkness listening intently to the creaking of the old house as it settled for the night, her breathing restrained as her fears rose at each sinister alarm that shivered through the building.

She started up in bed in the blackness pervading the room when an unnatural sound came from outside her window — an eerie scraping that caused her to suspect someone was climbing up in the shadows. Her heart pounded as fear spread through her. She gulped as tension caught in her throat, and then summoned up her courage and slipped out of bed to feel her way to the window.

Silvery moonlight bathed the ground in a blend of eerie light and heavy black shadows. Clasping her hands to her breast, Hester forced herself to gaze down into the indistinctness for movement. When she caught a glimpse of a figure walking slowly through the shrubbery her heart thumped painfully in her breast. Someone was prowling around out there. She shivered uncontrollably, and knew real fear as she watched intently.

She reminded herself that Hal and Lambert were going to patrol the grounds last thing, and tried to identify the elusive figure but failed. She watched its progress along a path leading to the rear of the house, and her heart lurched when another figure appeared out of the night from the opposite direction. The flash of a hooded lantern illuminated both figures, and Hester was certain one of the men was Hal. But the light was extinguished before she could be certain, and she watched in fearful anticipation as the figures turned and went along the path to disappear under the adjacent trees.

Hester did not forsake her position, although she began to feel chilled in the night air. Her gaze became accustomed to the gloom and she could see well to quite a distance. An hour passed unmeasured and her eyelids began to droop and feel heavy. Tiredness seeped into her and she felt a great need of sleep, but her fears remained vibrant, and she wondered if she would ever be able to rest normally again.

She was contemplating returning to

her bed when she saw furtive movement again, and stiffened. Two figures
materialised from the surrounding
darkness and began to steal silently
toward the house. She tried to identify
Hal's figure but failed, and watched in
horror as the men approached the front
wall of the building. They disappeared
in the dense shadows beneath her
window, and she strained her ears to
pick up unnatural sounds.

Moments passed, and then a harsh
voice called out a challenge. Hester
pressed close to the window, trying to
make out details. She saw the two men
running away from the house and at
that moment a pistol hammered echoingly and a reddish flash spurted
through the shadows. She gasped when
one of the fleeing men pitched to the
ground and lay still while the other kept
running to disappear into the shrubbery
of the garden.

A figure appeared from the left,
moving boldly, and she thought it was
Lambert. The butler paused beside the

inert figure and bent over to examine it. There was the flash of a lantern being unmasked, and dim light showed briefly before darkness swooped in again. Hester was aghast at the grim sight. One of the two interlopers had been shot before her very eyes!

She remained at the window and presently saw two men returning to the body on the grass, which was lifted and borne away. Then silence returned and the night resettled in its stillness. Hester sighed heavily. She was feeling deathly tired but sleep had been chased from her mind by the activity in the garden.

Later, she returned to her bed and lay in the close darkness staring into the blackness of the night, her nerves tense and alarm vibrant in the forefront of her mind. How long she lay in a state of high alert she did not know, but eventually she slept, and knew no more until sunlight peering in at the window struck her eyes and she stirred.

Her first thought was that she had been dreaming. She jumped out of bed and ran to the window. The sun was well above the horizon, its light enabling her to study the scene outside. There were no signs of the disturbance that had occurred during the night, and she gazed in horror at the spot where one of the intruders had fallen.

Daisy emerged from the dressing room, rubbing sleep from her eyes.

'Is everything all right, Miss?' she enquired, coming to the window.

Hester explained the sequence of nocturnal events and Daisy pressed closer to the window.

'I told you not to worry,' she observed. 'Master Hal is more than a match for any bad men.'

Hester was thoughtful as she prepared to face the new day. She performed her ablutions, and then endured the maid's attempts to brush her hair. When she was ready she made her way down to the front hall, and was pleased to see Hal there with Lambert. They were talking intently, and Hester, gazing at Hal and recalling the way he had kissed her, was suffused by a rush of warm emotion in her breast.

'Good morning, Hester.' Hal's voice was pitched low and his eyes were filled with warm regard. 'Did you sleep well?'

'I heard a commotion outside my window last night,' she responded, 'and was watching when that shot was fired.'

'I was hoping you did not witness that.' Hal glanced at the stolid Lambert. 'We were outside, and ready for any unlawful visitors. Two men did attempt to enter the house, but ran when Lambert challenged them. One was shot and injured. The other escaped. I'm waiting now for Jethro Scarfe to arrive.'

8

Hester felt confused as Hal led her into the dining-room to breakfast. He chatted as if he had not a care in the world, and Hester could only marvel at his self-possession, for her own mental stability was greatly upset.

She wondered about her feelings for Hal. He had kissed her and she had enjoyed it, but she was so weighted down by fearful anticipation she could not tell if she felt more than friendship toward him.

'How is the man who was shot during the night?' she asked, for the silence in the big room was intense and seemed greatly overpowering.

'He died just before dawn. Lambert went into Polgarron to get the doctor, but Spencer was out on a call and could not come. Lambert also informed the watchman that we had fought off intruders, and Scarfe will be along some time this morning.'

'And my father has not returned here?'

'No.' Hal shook his head. 'I expect he is busy in town. A desperate man like Jack Savage might find it simple to break out of gaol, and I expect Rufus is there to prevent such a possibility.'

Hester felt as if her surroundings were closing in upon her. She felt stifled, and longed for fresh air. Hal noted her distress and arose quickly.

'You're not looking very well,' he observed. 'Would you like to take a turn about the terrace for a few moments? It will be perfectly safe.'

'Yes, please.' Hester rose unsteadily to her feet and accompanied him to the front door.

Lambert was standing in the hall as if expecting callers. He frowned when he learned that they were going outside, and turned quickly to a table and picked up a pistol.

'Is that necessary?' Hester asked nervously.

'I'm afraid so.' Hal opened the door. 'Lambert will remain observant in the background. We cannot afford to take any chances.'

They went out to the terrace and Hester paused and breathed deeply of the sweet, refreshing air. The sun was warm on her shoulders.

'I was feeling quite overcome inside the house,' she said. 'I'm afraid my nerves are suffering.'

'It's not to be wondered at,' Hal sympathised. 'But this emergency will pass and then you'll be able to get on with your life.'

'You think I would be too easy a target standing still?' She forced a faint smile.

'It is better to keep all the odds on our side.' Hal's eyes were hard and sharp as he looked around. 'Your father is sending over two of his most trusted men this morning to act as guards around the house. You will be quite safe here.'

'I'm beginning to wish I had never left London.' Hester gazed at the landscape with critical gaze, although was enamoured by what she saw. She shook her head. 'I don't think I really mean that,' she added slowly. 'I shouldn't have wanted to miss any of this, and it is not my fault that Willard is Jack Savage.'

'I'm glad you decided to come here,' Hal said softly. 'My life was exceedingly dull until your arrival.'

'Really?' She looked into his eyes and saw an intense brightness in them.

'Yes.' He nodded. 'If it were not for you I should have missed this great adventure. You blundered into my life a week ago and now I am pledged to your service.'

'I'm very sorry it has turned out this way,' Hester apologised.

'Please don't be,' he begged. 'I believe in fate, and your arrival bears all the marks of divine intervention. I shouldn't dream of questioning it. We have been thrown together, and should face whatever comes.'

'And what about the risk to your life;

are you not afraid something bad might happen to you?'

He shook his head, smiling. 'I can only do what I think is right . . . There is much that is wrong with life these days, and every man must do his utmost to fight the forces of evil. I see much of the bad side of life, working as I do in the courts every day, and although much is being done to improve our lot, we still have a great deal more to do. I like to think that your coming into our midst has started something that will end the blight we have suffered recently from the likes of Jack Savage.'

Hester nodded agreement as they descended the terrace steps. Hal slipped an arm protectively around Hester's shoulders and they followed a path that led into the flower garden. Hester's spirits began to revive at their contact and she was somewhat disappointed when Lambert called to them from his vantage point at the top of the terrace steps.

'There's a rider coming, Master Hal,' the butler reported.

'Can you see who it is?' Hal countered.

'It looks like Jethro Scarfe. I'd know his style of riding anywhere.'

'We'd better get the business with him settled.'

Hester looked along the drive and saw a horseman approaching at a brisk pace.

'That's Jethro Scarfe,' Hal said. 'He's an officious man, very aware of his own importance, but fairly good at his thankless job. We shall do well to be rid of him within an hour. He will leave no stone unturned in his search for evidence.'

The rider dismounted at the bottom of the steps and a stable boy appeared as if from nowhere to take charge of the horse.

Scarfe was tall and thin; dressed severely in a black frock coat that reached almost to his knees. Silver buckles on his black shoes glittered in the sunlight. He mounted the steps slowly, stiffly, his long, lean face unsmiling. His dark eyes were expressionless, and caught and held Hester's gaze before he reached the top step. She found the power of his gaze hypnotic and stared at him like a rabbit mesmerised by a weasel.

'I'm glad you're here at last, Jethro,' Hal remarked. 'This is Hester Hendry.'

'How do you do, Mistress Hendry?' Scarfe doffed his hat. 'I can see your resemblance to Rufus. I would have been here much earlier but for Jack Savage's escape from the town jail just before dawn this morning.'

'He's escaped?' Hal gasped in disbelief.

'He has, and worse than that, he killed the gaoler and wounded Rufus, who tried to stop him.'

'My father is hurt?' Hester felt a thrill of horror stab through her beast and lifted a hand to her mouth. 'Is his life in danger?'

'I have the word of Doctor Spencer

that Rufus will pull through.' Scarfe shook his head. 'A pistol ball passed through his ribs but missed all vitals, and it will be only a matter of time before Rufus gets on his feet again. I shall take a statement from you, Miss Hendry, although it will be superfluous now. We know without doubt that Willard Cooper is Jack Savage. I have raised a hue and cry for him, but he is more devious than a wagonload of monkeys, and has many friends in this part of the country. I don't expect to apprehend him easily.'

'We have a dead man on our hands,' Hal said. 'He and another were trying to break into the house last night. When we challenged them they ran, and Lambert opened fire. One fell and the other escaped.'

'I'll take a look at him shortly,' Scarfe said. 'Let us go into the house and get down to business.'

Hal ushered Hester into the house, closely followed by Scarfe, and led the way into the dining-room. Hester made a statement under repeated questioning, and signed it when Scarfe was satisfied. Then Hal took Scarfe to view the body of the man who had been killed trying to break into the house. Hester waited for what seemed an eternity before Hal returned alone.

'Scarfe has gone,' he reported. 'Shall we go into town? I'm sure you will want to see Rufus.'

'Yes, please.' Hester arose quickly. 'I must go to my father.'

Polgarron was bustling with activity when they arrived. Fishing crafts were in the bay, already following their occupation. Seagulls were diving and swooping over the boats as nets were pulled in. Hester looked toward the building where she had been abducted the day before and a shiver racked her slim body.

But she was thankful for Hal's advent into her life, and a warm regard flared in her breast as she accompanied him to the doctor's door, which was opened by a tall, homely-looking woman who smiled and curtseyed when they were introduced.

'Mrs Spencer, the doctor's wife,' Hal said. 'This is Hester Hendry.'

Mrs Spencer grasped Hester's hands in welcome.

'It is so nice to meet you, Hester,' she declared, 'although this is not the best of situations, but Rufus is a strong man with a marvellous constitution, and Adam is certain he will pull through. He will allay any fears you might have about your father's condition.'

Hester liked Ada Spencer from the outset. The woman seemed so concerned about her husband's patients, as if she lived her life wrapped up in the doctor's work. She chatted to Hester as if she were a long-lost cousin as they entered the house, and Hester felt completely at ease by the time they entered a big room overlooking the bay, where Doctor Spencer was attending Rufus; who was lying inertly in a bed, his upper body swathed in bandaging.

'Adam, Hester has come to visit

Rufus,' Mrs Spencer declared. 'What is your latest report?'

Doctor Spencer looked up from taking Rufus's pulse. He smiled a greeting as he straightened from his patient, and his blue eyes twinkled with pleasure as he bent over Hester's hand.

'I've been expecting you, Miss Hendry,' he said. 'How are you feeling now? Rufus has been extremely lucky. The pistol ball missed his vitals, and all I have to concern myself about is infection. If we can get him through the next week or so then he will be out of danger.'

Hester gazed upon her father, who was barely conscious. Rufus looked stricken, lying inert and scarcely seeming to breathe. His face was pale with shock.

Hester took hold of her father's hand and Rufus half-opened his eyes. Unaccustomed emotion surged into Hester's breast and she blinked rapidly against a rush of tears.

'Father, it is I,' she said softly, chafing

his hand. 'How are you feeling now?'

Rufus looked up at her, his gaze unfocused, but a faint smile appeared on his lips and he sighed.

'Hester, I'm glad you've come. Don't worry about me. I can take this in my stride. Is Hal with you? He's got to be very careful until they've got Willard back behind bars. He shot me down in cold blood after his friends broke into the gaol, and he said he would kill you if it's the last thing he ever does.'

'Don't worry about Hester, Rufus,' Hal came to the bedside. 'I shall take very good care of her.'

'Dear Father,' she whispered. 'Please get well. We have so much to learn about each other. I was reluctant to come to Cornwall at first, but now I've met you nothing can make me leave.'

'He cannot hear you now,' Spencer said. 'He keeps slipping out of his senses. I shall keep a close watch on him for another day at least, and then I shall expect to see good signs of recovery.' He glanced at the attentive

Hal. 'Have they caught Willard Cooper yet, do you know?'

'Not as far as I know, Doctor,' Hal replied. 'I should think he is well away from here by now, or should be if he has any sense at all, but he does have many friends in these parts so there is no telling where he could be hiding.'

'They've put a price of fifty guineas on his head, dead or alive,' Spencer observed. 'That should restrict his circle of friends. Someone will certainly go for the reward. I expect Willard to be back in gaol in less than a week, and he won't get the chance to escape again . . .'

Hester took a lingering look at Rufus before turning away. Mrs Spencer ushered her to the door.

'I shall keep you informed of Rufus's progress,' Spencer called after her. 'No need to worry about him. He has the constitution of an ox. It would take more than a pistol ball to kill him.'

Hal's face was grim when they paused on the quay. He could see that

Hester was distressed, and wondered how best to occupy her to get through the rest of the day. He placed a hand upon her arm and Hester looked up at him with eyes that were shimmering with tears.

'Try not to worry about Rufus,' he said reassuringly. 'He is a man of immense strength, and the doctor is right when he says Rufus will pull through this. What we have to concern ourselves with is keeping you out of further trouble.'

'Thank you for taking so much trouble with my security,' Hester replied in a low tone. 'Perhaps I should return to London until this trouble is settled.'

'That may not be a good idea.' Hal shook his head. 'In London you would be alone, unprotected, but while you remain here you will have several good men around you, ready to defend you should Willard make an attempt on your life.'

Hester shook her head, unable to

decide what to do. She looked into Hal's intent face, saw warm regard in his eyes, and sensed the strength of his feelings, aware that he was ready to lay down his own life for her. But the knowledge filled her with trepidation. She did not want to be responsible for his death. Perhaps it would be better if she returned to London and lost herself in the masses living there until the danger Willard was posing had passed, either by his recapture or death.

Hal saw her indecision and tightened the clasp of his fingers upon her arm. The strength of his hand was reassuring, and she felt, in that moment, that she was unwilling to depart now she had met him. An indefinable attraction was seeping into her mind and nerve ends, filling her with emotion where, previously, none had existed. She placed a hand over his fingers on her arm and squeezed them gently.

'I shall stay here,' she said firmly. 'But please be very careful what you do, Hal. I should die if you suffered any mishap on my account.'

He smiled and nodded, satisfied with her decision, and helped her into the waiting coach. Lambert sprang out of the vehicle and mounted to sit beside the driver.

'Take us home,' Hal directed. 'We shall prepare for a trip to Halverstock. We'll leave this area until we hear that Jack Savage has been recaptured.'

Hester looked at him with enquiry in her eyes as he entered the coach and sat opposite her. He smiled.

'Halverstock is our house on the north coast,' he explained. 'You'll be quite safe there. I see no point in your remaining here while Rufus is unconscious. Your presence would serve no purpose and might enable Willard to get at you. I think it is the answer to our problems. I shall instruct a messenger to report to us each day with news of Rufus's progress.'

Hester did not object. She was overcome by the eternal vigilance that had to be maintained around her and the constant threat hanging over her head. She settled back in her seat and closed her eyes wearily, soothed by the gentle rocking of the coach as it followed the coach road.

Exhausted by the mental strain she was under, Hester was lulled into a soothing, semi-conscious state that drained her mind of cares, until Lambert shouted a harsh warning. Then a pistol shot rang out and a horse whinnied in pain. Hester opened her eyes as the coach suffered a tremendous impact that thrust it sideways with sickening force.

Hester clutched at the strap on her side as the coach slithered inexorably toward the steep precipice of the cliff on the right, half spinning around as grating sounds jarred heavily through the silence. Hal grasped Hester's hand to steady her while he attempted to open the coach door on his left.

There was a sudden lurch, and the coach tilted alarmingly as one large rear wheel slithered over the edge of the cliff. The vehicle came to rest at a frightening angle that tried to drag Hester into the lowest corner that was overhanging the cliff and, as her weight shifted across the centre of gravity, the whole coach teetered like a giant seesaw; seemingly about to plunge down into the swirling waves far below . . .

9

Hal threw open the coach door and leaned out of the aperture in an attempt to use his weight to counter-balance the sickening movement of the vehicle. His face was pale and drawn, and tension showed in his eyes.

'Don't move, Hester,' he commanded quietly. 'Just remain still; and do exactly as I say. We are perched on the edge of the cliff, and any change in the distribution of our weight could take us over the edge. Now, very slowly, try to pull yourself toward me using my hand; no sudden or jerky movements but a steady pull. Can you try that?'

Hester hardly dared to breathe. She could feel herself being drawn down into the lowest corner of the coach as it dipped over the edge of the cliff, and discovered that she was paralysed by fear and quite unable to move. A frightening tremor shook the coach and it seemed to slip an inch or two farther over the precipice.

'I need your weight up here beside me,' Hal encouraged. His right hand was holding the side of the coach above him while Hester grasped his outstretched left hand. He tried to draw her toward him but succeeded only in rocking the vehicle.

Hester tried to close her mind to the frightening thoughts that threatened to overcome her. The heart-stopping see-sawing motion of the coach set up a trembling in her breast, and for some moments she was unable to obey Hal's command while her mind screamed silently that she was about to die.

'You can do it, Hester,' Hal said firmly. 'Lean the upper part of your body toward me and try to move along the seat. A few inches will make all the difference.'

Hester looked up into his eyes. He was smiling encouragement, but she saw beads of perspiration on his brow.

She leaned across the intervening space between them and the coach rocked, dipping precariously. Fear rushed through her as graphic pictures of the sheer drop under her feet burst in her mind. She could hear stones and small rocks plunging over the edge of the cliff, dislodged by the coach, and her heart gave a great leap of fear.

'Master Hal, are you all right?' Lambert's voice, tense with fear, sounded just outside the coach, and the vehicle slithered a fraction more over the cliff as weight was applied to the front wheel that was still on firm ground as the butler stepped upon it.

'Keep your weight where you've just put it, Lambert,' Hal said quickly. 'That's fine. I've got Miss Hester by the hand and I'm endeavouring to draw her closer.'

The imbalance seemed to lessen with the butler's added weight. Hester drew a deep breath and restrained it as she prepared to make an effort. There were butterflies in her stomach and she closed her mind to the awful truth of their predicament. Hal increased his pressure on her left arm, which felt as if it was being dragged out of its socket, but she placed her right hand on the seat at her side and tried to lever herself toward safety. Now the coach remained steady and she gained a few precious inches.

'That's good,' Hal said through clenched teeth. 'Now make another try, Hester. You are doing very well. I'm going to transfer my grip to your wrist and then I shall want you to grasp the side of the coach with your fingers and hold on while I clasp you around the waist. Then I'll be able to lift you higher.'

Hester dared not reply. Hal began to draw her up, and a few inches sufficed to enable her to clamp her fingers around the door post of the coach. Hal shifted his grip to her shoulder and eased her higher toward safety, and Hester swung her right hand across her body and secured a second grip on the door post. Hal gradually hauled her upward, and she released her hold on the side of the coach as he threw his weight backwards out of the doorway, taking her bodily with him as he fell off the vehicle. Their concerted movement caused the coach to slip away on its knife-edge.

Hal landed on his back with Hester atop him, and quickly gained his feet to pull her away from the edge of the cliff. Hester's legs refused to take her weight and Hal lifted her and moved to safety. Lambert jumped clear of the coach and, as the butler got to his feet the vehicle lurched and then plunged noisily amid a shower of stones over the sheer drop and into the cove.

Hester was trembling uncontrollably. Hal held her in a close embrace, supporting her and making soothing noises.

'The horses!' she gasped. 'What happened to them?'

'A boulder was rolled down the slope above us. It smashed the shafts of the coach and the horses bolted.' Lambert came to Hal's side. 'I fired a shot when I saw two men pushing the rock down on us, and then Belcher, the driver, and I, had to jump for our lives. Belcher went off along the road after the horses, and didn't stop when I called him back to help with the coach.'

'You saw two men pushing that boulder?' Hal demanded.

'And recognised one of them,' Lambert replied tensely. 'It was George Bowdler, one of Willard's close friends, and I think I nicked him with a pistol ball before he ducked out of sight.'

'Perhaps you'll go up the slope and check,' Hal suggested, and Lambert nodded and went off with a pistol in his hand.

'How are you feeling now?' Hal enquired solicitously of Hester.

Hester straightened. Hal's arms were around her, strong and comforting, and he eased his grip for her to stand without aid, but she staggered, and he slid a reassuring arm around her waist.

Hester clung to him.

'I can hardly get my breath,' she replied shakily.

'It was an experience I should not wish to repeat,' Hal observed. 'You're trembling, Hester. Let us start walking back to Polgarron. The exercise should relieve your shock.'

They set out at a slow walk back toward the town. Hester stayed as far as she could from the cliff edge, and Hal held her arm tightly. They sat down to rest after covering a mile, and Lambert caught up with them. The butler was grim-faced. He was holding a pistol in his hand and there was another in his belt. He seemed very alert as he confronted them.

'No signs of anyone back there,' he reported. 'But I did find blood stains on the grass. I'll report the matter to Jethro Scarfe when we get back to town. Shall I go on ahead, Master Hal? I could get a carriage and come to pick you up. Miss Hester looks completely done in.'

'That's a good idea, Lambert.' Hal nodded.

'Perhaps you'll take one of my pistols,' Lambert suggested. 'You never know who might show up after what has happened.'

Hal took the proffered pistol and Lambert set off at a fast pace along the road to town. Hester arose and Hal grasped her arm.

'We could stay here until Lambert returns if you don't feel up to walking,' he suggested.

'I think we should go on,' Hester replied firmly.

Hal smiled encouragingly. 'It's a strange thing, but before your arrival I was feeling that life was comparatively dull, and in the week that I've known you my well-ordered day-to-day business has been turned around completely.'

'And all these mishaps are down to me. I'm so sorry, Hal. If you hadn't been afoot on the road when I almost walked into the smugglers after the coach was held up, none of this would have happened.'

'I wouldn't have missed it for anything,' he rejoined. 'And it's an odd thing, but it doesn't seem as if we are comparative strangers. You have captured my imagination and I am intrigued. I feel as if I have known you all my life.'

Hester looked into his eyes and Hal smiled. They were standing very close together and he slid both arms around her in a comforting embrace. Hester allowed her head to rest on his broad shoulder. She heard him sigh. Her breathing became unsteady and a strange throbbing started in her temples. Her legs trembled so badly that Hal had to support her. She felt his cheek touching her face and put her arms around him, clinging to him as if her life depended upon their contact. Hal pressed his lips against her hair, and Hester closed her eyes.

The sound of wheels grating on hard ground, accompanied by the beat and thud of hoofs, finally alerted them and

Hal turned swiftly in the direction of the sound. An open carriage was coming toward them, being driven by a young man who was whipping the two-horse team and urging it along at a break-neck pace. Hal grasped Hester's arm and led her into the cover of a nearby pile of rocks. He peered out at the approaching carriage.

'It's Tom Tremain,' he observed. 'Rufus introduced you to him in The Fisherman's Arms. He always drives at that reckless pace. One of these days he'll go over the cliff, if he isn't more careful. You'd be wise not to take a ride with him, Hester.'

'I shouldn't want to ride with anyone but you,' she responded warmly, and was rewarded with a quick smile.

Tremain hauled on his reins when he saw them, and stopped his team within feet of where they stood, the matched pair of greys snorting and gasping from their efforts.

'I saw your man back there and he told me what had happened,' Tremain said. 'I've sent him on to town to tell Jethro Scarfe, and came as quickly as I could to pick you up.'

'That's kind of you, Tom,' Hal observed. 'But under the circumstances I must refuse your offer. Hester has had enough mishaps since her arrival in Cornwall without inviting more by travelling with you.'

Tremain laughed and reached into a pocket of his coat. He lifted a small pistol into view and cocked it as he pointed the black muzzle in their direction.

'I insist that you accompany me,' he said harshly, his smile vanishing. 'You will drive, Hal, and we'll head for my home on Tavis Point. A close friend of mine is hiding there, and he'll be very pleased to see Hester, so come and join me and we'll be on our way, but discard your pistol, Hal, or I shall be forced to shoot you dead on the spot.'

'Are you joking?' Hal demanded.

'Not at all! Willard is a close friend of mine and I must help him out of his present situation.'

'To the extent of committing murder?' Hal stepped in front of Hester.

'Don't be a fool, Hal,' Tremain urged. 'I am an excellent shot, and it would be too easy for me to kill you and roll your body off the cliff. Willard wants Hester, and I intend taking her to him. You are surplus to Willard's requirements, and I shall have no hesitation in disposing of you.'

'Do as he says, Hal,' Hester said quietly. 'Don't get yourself killed.'

Hal paused for what seemed an eternity with Tremain pointing his deadly-looking pistol at him, and then he sighed and released his hold on the pistol in his right hand.

'That's better,' Tremain observed. 'Now come and climb in. You drive, Hal, while I sit in the back with Hester. Willard will be mightily pleased to see her.'

'Are you prepared to deliver her to him, knowing full well that he will surely murder her?' Hal demanded.

'I'm afraid that is the way it will be.'
Tremain nodded.

Hal handed Hester into the carriage
and then mounted to the driving seat.
Tremain joined Hester and sat beside
her, his pistol pointing at Hal's back.
Hal picked up the reins and urged the
horses into motion and they continued
along the cliff top to Tavis Point, where
a lone mansion stood silhouetted
against the pale sky, lonely and hostile.

'There's nothing personal in my
attitude,' Tremain said pleasantly, 'but
one must always do what one can to
help a friend in need.'

'And you are one of his criminal
associates,' Hester countered.

'Quite so. I have aided Willard in
holding up several coaches. It has
proved to be quite exciting and
profitable.'

'You won't get away with this,
Tremain,' Hal said over his shoulder.
'My man Lambert knows you've come
to pick us up, and when it is learned
that we have disappeared Jethro Scarfe

will put two and two together and you will quickly find yourself under arrest.'

'Save your breath,' Tremain retorted. 'I lied when I said I'd sent Lambert on to Polgarron to report to Scarfe. When he told me what had happened to your coach I shot him and rolled him off the cliff. No-one knows that I have picked you up, and your disappearance will remain a mystery.'

Hester gasped in shock. Hal fell silent. The carriage swayed and jolted along the cliff top as it bore them inexorably towards Willard waiting at Tavis Point . . .

10

Hester was frozen in fear, unable to assimilate the dreadful news that Lambert had been murdered. Tremain was smiling coldly, his features stiff with determination.

Hal kept glancing over his shoulder at them, his expression harsh, eyes narrowed in desperation, but with Tremain's pistol pointed at his back there was nothing he could do about the situation.

The cliff road forked to the right and Hal took the fork to follow the meandering path toward Tavis Point. They passed between two massive black iron gates and followed a twisting drive through a plantation of elms and poplars.

Hal swung the team around a sharp bend in the path and the carriage tilted sharply to the right, throwing Tremain to one side. Hester launched herself at him while he was unbalanced. Her left hand grasped his right wrist and she thrust his hand and the pistol it held up in the air and threw her right arm around Tremain's neck and clung to him with all her desperate strength.

'Hal,' she screamed. 'Help me.'

The carriage halted so abruptly that Hester and Tremain were thrown to the floor of the vehicle. Hester concentrated her efforts to retain a hold on Tremain's right wrist. She clung to him desperately until Hal came plunging off the driving seat and joined the struggle. Tremain proved no match for Hal and was quickly disarmed. Hal struck Tremain with his fist and Tremain subsided and lay inert.

Hester sank back weakly on a seat and gazed at Hal, who picked up Tremain's discarded pistol. He came to her side, his face showing anxiety.

'Are you all right?' he asked. 'That was a very brave thing you did.'

'I had nothing to lose,' Hester

replied. 'We were both facing death.'

'We must get away from here.' Hal pocketed the pistol and then pushed Tremain out of the carriage. 'We need to get back to Polgarron.'

'Shouldn't we take Tremain with us and hand him over to Jethro Scarfe?'

'We should, but I'm not taking any more chances. Willard is around here, I've no doubt.'

Hal climbed back into the driving seat and took up the reins. Hester gazed at Tremain's inert body as the carriage was turned, and she saw him begin to stir as Hal drove back the way they had come. But her relief was short-lived. When they came in sight of the big black gates she saw that they had been closed, and two men were walking along the driveway toward them.

Hal stopped the team and gazed at the approaching men.

'One of them is Willard!' he gasped. 'And he's got Barney Kepple with him!'

Hester recognised the big man accompanying Willard as being one of the two who had abducted her on the quay in Polgarron.

'Turn the carriage,' she gasped. 'Drive fast, Hal, and they won't catch us. We must get back to town.'

Hal needed no urging. He swung the team around and sent the carriage back along the drive, urging the horses into a gallop. Willard and Kepple broke into a run but were soon left behind, and Tremain had to leap for his life when the carriage whirled around a bend and bore down upon him. Hal whipped the horses into their best efforts and Hester clung for dear life to the side of the swaying vehicle.

Hal veered to the right and turned away from the big house. They rapidly approached the cliff edge, and Hal swung the team to follow a path that led in the direction of the distant town. Hester looked over her shoulder, and was relieved when she saw no sign of pursuit.

Eventually they reached a tall fence that barred their further progress, and

Hal brought the team to a halt.

'It looks as if we shall have to continue on foot,' he said. 'Do you feel up to it, Hester?'

'Is there an alternative?' she countered.

Hal nodded reassuringly. 'Don't give up hope yet. We are far from done. Come on, we must climb over the fence. There's a footpath on the other side that will take us right into Polgarron.'

'We are too late,' Hester said. 'Willard and Kepple are coming on horses.'

Hal looked in the direction Hester was pointing and his expression turned bleak when he saw two riders approaching at a furious gallop.

'They'll have to chase us on foot if we get over the fence,' he remarked.

He grasped Hester's arm and they left the carriage. The fence was six feet high and looked to be a formidable obstruction, but Hal lifted Hester bodily, thrust her upward, and as she grasped the top of the fence a shot rang out, shattering the silence.

Hal lifted Hester to her feet and urged her to run. They hurried along the cliff path toward Polgarron, but Hester felt a sharp pain in her left ankle — she had landed awkwardly over the fence. Hal soon noticed her distress and looked around in some desperation but there was nowhere they could hide.

'I'm sorry, Hal,' Hester gasped. 'My ankle! I can't go on.'

'Then we must face them here,' he said grimly, examining the pistol he had taken from Tom Tremain. 'I have just one shot. Let us find a spot where you can rest. There's a little hollow just ahead, and that should give you some cover.'

Hester tried to hurry but her ankle was swelling painfully and she could only hobble to the depression near the edge of the cliff. She dropped into it with a sigh of relief, and was entirely out of sight when she lay flat.

'Stay down, Hester,' he directed. 'I

doubt if Kepple has any shots left. He's fired at us, and hasn't had time to reload his pistol.'

Hester did not reply. She closed her eyes and a prayer came to her lips. She had feared that this was how it would end — Willard or his men closing in like wild predators, intent on murdering her. Only Hal stood between her and certain death, and she wondered what particular fate had thrown them together, and why they were being forced to face this violent end.

'Hal,' she gasped. 'You could get away. Save yourself.'

'I chose to make it my business,' he replied firmly. 'Anyone wanting to kill you will have to go through me. I shall stand my ground, Hester.'

Hester fell silent, unable to argue against his determination, aware that he was prepared to die for her. She watched Kepple approaching. Hal remained motionless, the pistol in his right hand down at his side.

'You've led us a merry dance,'

Kepple shouted as he came closer. 'But I've got you now.'

He produced a pistol as he spoke, and levelled it at them. Hal raised his pistol, and Hester heard an ominous click as it was cocked.

There was further movement at the fence, and Hester saw with fading hope that Willard and Tom Tremain were climbing over it. Kepple drew even nearer, and then halted; his face contorted. He was breathless from running and his shoulders heaved as he took aim at Hal, who was motionless and obdurate.

Hester closed her eyes, unable to watch, but the sound of a pistol forced her to look again, and she saw a cloud of black smoke surrounding Kepple's head and shoulders. Hal fell back a step in response, and Hester was horrified to see a patch of blood spreading through Hal's coat near the left shoulder.

The muzzle of Hal's pistol lifted slightly, like the nose of a hunting dog sniffing out game, and then the weapon exploded and smoke flared around Hal. Kepple uttered a shout of agony, spun around sharply under the strike of the pistol ball, and then dropped to his hands and knees. He paused for an interminable moment before falling inertly on his face.

Hal dropped the pistol and sat down heavily on the grass. His face was ghastly as he pressed his hand to the bloodstain on his left shoulder. Hester sprang up and went to his side, ignoring the pain in her ankle. When she tried to look at his wound, Hal shook his head.

'No time for that,' he said through clenched teeth. 'Go and check Kepple for shot and powder, and fetch his pistol. I need to reload before Willard and Tremain arrive.'

Hester hobbled to where Kepple was lying, her anxious gaze on the fence. Willard and Tremain were running towards them, and she could see that Willard at least was armed. She dropped to her knees beside Kepple, who was dead with a wound in his chest. Her hands trembled as she searched him and collected a powder horn and a small box that rattled when she shook it. She picked up the discarded pistol and ran painfully back to where Hal was sitting, her breath rasping in her throat.

It was a nightmare to watch Hal reloading Kepple's pistol. Willard and Tremain were approaching steadily, and Willard was shouting.

Hester dropped to the ground. She watched the approach of Willard and Tremain, unable to avert her gaze. Tremain was slightly to Willard's rear, and did not seem to possess a pistol. Willard came on until he was barely ten yards away and then raised his right hand, and Hester cringed at the sight of the big pistol levelling in their direction.

But Hal did not give Willard time to take aim. Hester flinched as Hal fired, and she saw Willard jerk under the impact of a pistol ball. Willard's pistol exploded, but the muzzle was still pointing at the ground, and then

Willard dropped limply and lay still. To Hester's great relief, Tom Tremain turned and fled. She hurried to Hal's side and bent over him.

'Willard is getting up,' Hal said sharply, and Hester looked over her shoulder to see Willard staggering to his feet. Blood was staining his shirt front, but he lurched forward in their direction, his hands outstretched toward Hester. 'Run, Hester,' Hal urged. 'Get away from here.'

'I won't leave you!' Hester stood frozen in horror, and then bent swiftly and picked up the pistol Hal had dropped, although she knew it was empty. She stood over Hal to defend him despite his protests. Willard approached. He was close to the edge of the cliff and staggered at each step.

Hester sprang at him as he came within an arm's length, raising the pistol to strike him. He laughed and dashed the weapon from her hand, and the next instant he had grasped her with merciless hands.

'I said I'd get you!' he gasped. 'I should have put you over the cliff when you told me you knew my secret.'

Hester struggled as he lifted her bodily. They were only a few feet from the cliff edge, and he lurched forward to carry out his threat.

Hal snatched up the pistol Hester had dropped and staggered to his feet. He swung the empty weapon and struck Willard on the back of the head. The highwayman staggered and then swung round to face the attack. He released his right hand from Hester but remained holding her with his left hand, and pushed her inexorably toward the edge of the cliff.

Hester felt her right foot slip over the edge of the precipice and clung to Willard's arm in frantic desperation as he tried to release his hold on her. Hal struck again with the pistol, and smashed the metal barrel against Willard's wrist, breaking his hold on Hester. He struck again, a shrewd blow that took Willard squarely in the face.

Willard reared back, lost his balance, and tottered on the cliff edge. Hester released her grip on him and he uttered a trailing cry of despair as his feet found nothing but thin air and he went plunging down to the obdurate rocks at sea level.

Hester was swaying over the cliff, her hands clutching desperately as momentum pulled her over the brink. Hal ignored the pain in his shoulder and grasped her around the waist, setting his feet on the grass and throwing his weight backward. For a terrifying moment he felt that they were too far gone, but his heavier weight prevailed and he fell back on firm ground, dragging Hester with him. They rolled on the grass on the very edge of the long drop to the rocks.

Hester lay within the circle of Hal's arms, her eyes closed tightly, and shudders racked her slender body. Her shock receded slowly, and when she finally opened her eyes she saw that Hal was watching her, a smile upon his lips.

She clung to him with all the fervour she could muster.

'I think we've put an end to the threat against your life,' he said in a matter-of-fact tone, but his face was set grimly and his eyes were alight with passion. 'We'd better start thinking about getting back to Polgarron.'

'I could stay here forever,' Hester whispered, clinging to him, 'if I could remain in your arms. You were so brave, Hal.'

'I had something worthwhile to fight for.' His good arm tightened around her waist, and it was the most natural thing in the world for Hester to tilt her face toward him.

Hal looked into her eyes, saw invitation in their depths, and kissed her. Hester embraced him as if she would never let him go again. They had been thrown together from the first moment they met, and she had no intention of fighting against her fate.

Eventually, Hal got to his feet and they walked back to the fence. They surmounted that final obstacle and climbed into Tremain's waiting carriage to return to Polgarron like a couple out for an afternoon drive. Hester was aware that it would take time for the shock and dangers attendant to her arrival to recede in her mind, but the nightmare was over, and the promise of a bright future beckoned as if fate had at last relented in their favour . . .

THE END

We do hope that you have enjoyed reading this large print book.

Did you know that all of our titles are available for purchase?

We publish a wide range of high quality large print books including:
Romances, Mysteries, Classics
General Fiction
Non Fiction and Westerns

Special interest titles available in large print are:
The Little Oxford Dictionary
Music Book, Song Book
Hymn Book, Service Book

Also available from us courtesy of Oxford University Press:
Young Readers' Dictionary
(large print edition)
Young Readers' Thesaurus
(large print edition)

For further information or a free brochure, please contact us at:
Ulverscroft Large Print Books Ltd.,
The Green, Bradgate Road, Anstey,
Leicester, LE7 7FU, England.
Tel: (00 44) **0116 236 4325**
Fax: (00 44) **0116 234 0205**

SECOND TIME AROUND

Margaret Mounsdon

Widowed single parent Elise Trent thought no one could replace her husband Peter, until she met policeman Mark Hampson. She is forced to seriously re-think her life when her mother-in-law Joan accepts a proposal of marriage from long time companion Seth Baxter, and her student daughter Angie and Mark's son Kyle get involved with an action group. Then Elise and Mark are further thrown together by a spate of country house burglaries . . .

SHACKLED TO THE PAST

Teresa Ashby

Midwife Laura Morgan moves in next door to Dr Steve Drake with her daughter, Abby. Steve had lost his wife and daughter when both were drowned. He becomes very fond of Abby and Laura begins to fall in love with him. But as the truth about the deaths of Steve's wife and child unfolds it seems that a happy future for them may never be possible, as long as he is haunted by the ghosts from the past.

THE BRIDE, THE BABY AND THE BEST MAN

Liz Fielding

In three weeks' time, Faith Bridges will marry safe, dependable, practical Julian. Their plans don't include children — just a nice, calm, platonic marriage. But then along comes Harry March, one adorable baby, and one cute four-year-old. Harry is definitely not safe — he's sexy, rude, impractical and utterly charming. He might have been best man material, but he isn't Faith's type at all . . . And as soon as she can stop herself kissing Harry she will tell him so!